JAY M LONDO

TRAPPED

INSIDE

Robert Hummel owned a business that built fallout shelters all around the world. And he had managed to make a fortune in doing so. His company decided to branch out and convert a 1960's abandon missile silo complex, into a very luxury condo nuclear bunker, built for the ultra-rich. He ended up selling each one for several million dollars. No money was spared in building his ultra-luxury complex.

A year after finishing and selling all the condos. it suddenly had looked like World War Three was about to seriously break out. So, all the rich owners fled to the safety of the fallout shelter to selfishly save themselves. Once they were safely inside. The blast doors then automatically had closed. They then physically couldn't be opened back up again for five-long years.

In the beginning it was like an extended vacation for all the residents locked up inside, life was really good. But that was not to last, over time, it felt like the walls were closing in all round on them. Slowly as time marched on for five long grueling years, it began to feel like an eternity to be forced to be locked up. And things began going really horribly wrong. And what was to come, couldn't be stopped. It was much too late for that now.

About a year or so in, people started to die for various different reasons. Some it was self-inflicted, some not by choice. The dynamics of being trapped inside for that long, unable to get out, weighed extremely heavy on each one of them. Its effects manifested differently in each of them, their mental states. It began crushing their souls. Rotting them from the inside out. At this point it was now survival of the fittest.

If that wasn't bad enough, then the food had started running out much too early. Then the starvation started setting in. It was at this point that the true madness had broken out amongst all of them. Humanity broke down.

There was seventy-eight residents in the beginning. The question was, were any of them actually going to actually be able to survive up until the very end? When the blast doors were slated to open up once more. With each day, humanity broke down just a bit more. They either would all end up starving to death, or perhaps killing one another. The people that they were when they fled to the safety of the shelter, was forever changed by their extended stay in what they began to realize, was to become their own private hell! Karma has a funny way of rearing its ugly head.

CHAPTER ONE:

"Grand Idea"

"Hey Joe, could you please come up to my office."

"You wanted to see me?"

Yes, come on in, hey shut the door would you, and then sit down please, you know Joe, Events around the world really have been going pretty shitty in the world as of late, the last couple of years. With covid, and all the craziness taking place around the world now. And it's certainly helping our sells. So, this then got me thinking really hard how we could capitalize on this even more than we already are. Then it had dawned on me. We need to do something much bigger, capitalize big time on all this kayos. So, this got me thinking, that we should at least try and protect ourselves. Especially if Putin stupid enough to go ahead and start a nuclear war. And what's the harm if we make some real money out of all the fear that's presently out there.

So little brother I know your think that this is going to sound absolutely ridiculous at first! But I have one hell of an idea for a new direction for our company to take. So please hear me out first before you cast judgment on the idea, alright."

"Go ahead and tell me, do you think that I will need a drink to hear this so-called grand idea of yours? I can tell that this is one of those hair brain ideas of yours, isn't?"

"Yes, you probably should, you should probably have a double. Ok go ahead and make us both one while you're at it."

"Ok so I've have had a couple sips, ok, go ahead rip the bandage off, go ahead and lay it on me, and tell me what this grand idea of yours is. And exactly just how much money is it going to end up costing me? Because your ideas always cost me money in the beginning."

"Are company has made a fortune since 911 selling fallout shelters, all around the world. I'm tired of just building our small shelters. I want to think much bigger than all this, something so large and so massive, A shelter large enough that it could actually house around seventy-five people for upwards of five years if needed. And survive and withstand a direct hit by a 10-kilo ton nuclear explosion.

Joe nearly chocked on his drink upon hearing this.

"Wait theirs more, and it needs to be completely self-sustaining. Calm down little brother, don't give that condescending look of yours, just hear me out first. I know that look of yours. So, if we can manage to pull this off. We could actually make luxury condo units for the rich. In are nuclear bunker. And sell them at top dollar, I'm talking for millions a piece. I'm still working on the numbers. But I was thinking between the three-to-seven-million-dollar range per condo. But it then gets even better on top of all that, we can then charge the owners a yearly fee to maintain the facility 24-7. So that everything is always up and ready to go, on a moment's notice. Around half a million-dollar fee per year for a minimum say perhaps ten years' time.

I'm talking about a bunker that is truly strong enough to be able to withstand a direct ten-kilo ton thermo-nuclear direct blast! Large enough to grow food, and produce its own water, and breathable air, and power. Not only that, but we would also offer a whole lot of feature comforts. I want the residents to be completely comfortable, things one wouldn't expect to be inside a nuclear bunker. All the feature comforts of home, and then some."

"What the hell, what you're now talking about would cost us millions to actually build! We don't have that kind of money to invest in something like that."

True, but we'll be making a fortune, and we can each get a unit for each of us and are families out of the deal. But I'm still working out all the details."

"How is this even going to be possible, you're talking about a whole lot of upfront construction cost. And where would we build this grand idea of yours?"

"Joe, what if I told you that we already purchased a piece of land which just happens to have a decommissioned Atlas missile silo complex that sits on twenty acres. Ninety miles northeast of Wichita Kansas. Out in the middle of nowhere."

"Wait just a minute! How in the hell much did that cost us? And I can't fucking believe that you didn't tell me about this before you just went ahead and bought it without consulting me first.

Don't you think it would have been nice to tell me first. I am your business partner."

"Well, here's the best part of it, $380,000!"

"Seriously, that's all you paid for it?"

"Yes, I got a hell of a deal on it, it was a government auction, but to get such a deal, well I had to act quickly. So, let me tell you about what we bought for $380,000. it's a large complex, there is two blast doors. Each one of these doors, each weigh more than seventy-five thousand pounds. The complex is more than two-hundred feet deep straight into the ground. The concrete walls are twelve feet thick, with reinforced concrete. There is already an underground well in place for fresh drinking water. I had a report on the water. It's really excellent quality water. Especially after we add modern day filtration system. There are five missile silos, and a command silo, that are all inter-connected by tunnels in between the silos. Each silo is more than seven thousand square feet, then there is a large command, and living space that is more the five thousand square feet. That's more than thirty-nine thousand square feet to work with. You might say that we have a blank slate to do with what we will.

Once the plans are completed. We will hire a marketing firm to produce rendering and videos of what the facility is going to look like once it's all complete. So, to actually help us fiancé the project we will start by taking pre-sales of the different condos which will range in size and price range. This will allow the purchasers to be able to select the design and finishes of their own units. And even before they are allowed to select and purchase a unit. They must first pass our financial requirements just to even be considered. They must be at least worth a minimum of fifty million dollars net worth. We need to be sure that they can actually afford the cost of their condo, and the half a million-dollar yearly fee to keep everything up and running, always completely ready. And they must also pass a criminal background check. So, what do you think of my plan now little brother?"

"Actually, I am quite impressed! This is actually a really promising idea."

"Well, I'm glad to hear you say that. Because this is going to become a whole new branch of our company. I'll going to be remaining the C.E.O of both companies, But I actually want you to be in charge of the day-to-day operation of our core business. I want to be able to focus much more of my attention on this new venture. So, what do you say little brother, you ready to step up to the big league, I know you can do this, and of course you will also own forty percent of the new company, And I think with you promotion how about a twenty-five thousand dollar raise per year. What do you say bro you want in?

"Hell, yes, I'm in! Thanks, we are going to make a fortune on this, aren't we?

"Absolutely, I'll tell you what. I was really hoping that you would feel this strongly about this. I have already arranged it. We are going to be flying out to the site tomorrow morning. I want to show it to you. Go home and pack, we're going to be gone for two days. I'll pick you up at 4am, so be ready, I'm not going to wait for you."

We will be landing in Wichita around nine the tomorrow morning. From there I hired a helicopter to then fly us both out to the sight. Are new guy, that I had hired for security will be meeting us out there and show us both around. Along with an architect, and an engineer, and the contractor that I have hired for the build out the complex. I'm also having the gal that I hired to sell the condo's all meeting us at the airport. Then we will all be flying out to the site together. Last week we set up an office on site, and also brought out several living trailers for the workers to stay out at the site while its under construction. And large generators for all the power needs.

CHAPTER TWO:

"Out On Site"

My brother and I had ended up being the last to arrive at the Wichita airport. But the others hadn't been waiting for very long for us thankfully. Everybody else was already aboard the helicopter. It was a thirty-minute flight out from the airport. Being early spring there was still a bit of snow that was on the ground. Luckily, it was a sunny day.

Once we had landed at our new sites, I went ahead and then introduced everyone to Joe. Our new head of security Dave Becker was there to great us after we had landed. He's tall, and a broadly built guy. He has extensive military background, and he's an expert on security. Including setting up state of the art security equipment. His first task is to vet anyone working on the project. Installing a state-of-the-art fence around the entire twenty acres. Which includes a whole lot of cameras, and ground sensors. We needed to keep the secrets of this place from the public. I don't want a bunch of people knowing what we are doing here.

We all disembarked from the helicopter. Then the Helicopter headed back out. Then I began.

"Well, I would like to thank you all for coming out here today. I would like to first go ahead and introduce you all to my business partner, and brother Joe.

Joe smiled and said, "Thank you for all coming out here today."

"Joe this is our architect, Jeff Cock, he has made a career in designing both military, and civilian fallout bunkers. When I told him what I had in mind, he got quite intrigued."

Joe reached out, and shock Jeffs hand. "It's a pleasure meeting you, I look forward to seeing your plans for our little project here."

Then I introduced the engineer I hired to design all the systems that we will need to keep this place going. This is Chad Johnston." Joe shuck his hand.

"Joe I would like to introduce you to Jack Sampson, our new general contractor. He's going to be building our little project for us. And Jeff and

Jack, and Chads have been working together for years. They really know their stuff. That's why I had hired them."

And last but not least, I would like to introduce you to Cindy Van Dyk. She specializes in interior design and selling of very unique real estate such as this. As I had introduced her, she had a great big smile painting on her face. I hadn't noticed before, that she has really beautiful big green eyes. I had lost my train of thought for a moment. She must be casting some sort of a spell on me.

Joe then said, "Thank you all for coming out here today."

Dave then went ahead and piped in, could you all please follow me over to the office. We can have you drop your stuff at your rooms. Plus, I have gear ready for all of you to go in and see the complex. The good news is it's now all completely dry in the sight, we pumped it all out last week. And I have lights set up. So, I have hard hats for you all to wear for safety.

We all then headed over to the blast door entrance. The blast doors were wide open. We all walked inside. Coming into the living, and command center portion first. The old control stations from the sixties still was in place. But what was really cool was standing at the bottom of the abandoned silo and then glancing straight up. It was a very long ways back up, as tall as a twenty-story building. Standing there, it really gives you the feeling of just how large this place truly is. And the amount of area that we have to work with. It was the same height of a twenty-story building. That's damn tall.

Chad wanted to see the well and the water pump. He spent several minutes taking notes. And evaluating the rate of flow of water. Then he finally spoke up. Well, a couple of things come to mind. I'm suggesting that we should dig a secondary well. And dig it deep. This would be a geothermal hole. The idea is we would inject water down the shaft that we dug. The natural hot temps of the ground would then heat the water up thru natural forces. Then the steam that was being produced would then come up a second shaft and would come up as steam. Then with the steam. I could design a system that would provide all the hot water needs for this facility, and in addition to that it could be used to provide all the hot water. The steam also could be used to then turn a turbine that could then produce a constant stream of electrical power 24 hours a day. It would be a constant power source, but we would also install Tesla house batteries, for emergency backup. By doing this, you wouldn't have to rely solely on a generator, and all the fuel to run the massive generator, and dealing with the harmful exhaustion the generator would then end up being produced, while running. It would end up producing. Initially it would be quite an expensive on upfront cost, but operating cost would be nearly zero once it was up and running. Then just like a nuclear submarine, I could then produce the oxygen from the water itself, we would still have to filter all the air and scrub the carbon oxide back out the air being breathed in the complex. So, the oxygen could both be produced, and recycled.

I was blown away this was next level stuff about which he was talking about here. Ok I like it, if you would work up a design, and a cost to install this. I would be very much interested in this. It's really a good idea.

Jeff, I want to let you know what I was thinking we should do for the design. Three of the silo's would house all the condos. I would like each story to be minimum of ten feet tall. Make things appear to be bigger, not as confining. The fourth silo would be used for storage, and for food growing. The fifth silo would be for entertainment. And the control silo would become are new control center, storage, and house the equipment rooms. And additional food growing. From there, I would like to see what you all end come up with.

"Ms. Van Dyk what kinds of luxuries do you feel that should be incorporated into the overall design."

"Well considering that you want the cliental to be ultra-wealthy. And there is a chance the residences could be locked in the bunker for upwards of five years, then the bunker should include these amenities. And plus, it will make the bunker more markable, and fetch more money for each unit. a luxurious movie theater room, a great room for group gatherings, with a small kitchen, a bar, exercise room, which would include weightlifting, and yoga, and dance rooms, with showers, combination small court that could be used for basketball, and volleyball, pickle ball, tennis. Sun tanning room so people can still get their vitamin D, a gaming room, public bathrooms, I know this sounds crazy, but I think a whole floor where we install a pound and plant lots of tropical plants, it would be a small connection to the outside world. A swimming pool, hot tub, and sauna. Also, a craft room, and a library sitting room. And a medical room. There needs to be a lot of plant, and small trees in all the communal areas, and a whole lot of electronic windows, in addition each silo, and entertainment area should all have elevators. We don't won't the owners to feel like they are living in a prison, but more of a luxury grand hotel. You install these amenities, and I should be able to get at least an additional million-in-half, to two million more per unit." When Cindy was done talking, I happened to notice that she looked directly over at me. It was important for her to know what I had thought of her idea's.

"Well Jeff what do you think can we do this?"

"I think she's absolutely right. I'll figure it out."

"Well first of all, I would like to thank everyone for coming here today. This was a very productive meeting I would say. I'm so excited by this project. And Jack I can't wait for you to be building out my dream. I liked all the ideas that you have all proposed to us. Joe as my business partner, what do you think? Without your approval, we won't move forward, partners right.

"Well, I think that my brother and I, would like to move forward with your ideas. We would like your firm to move forward, with the designing this complex, And Chad it sounds like you have a whole lot of systems to now design. We want this place state of the art in every way possible. I think everything should be automated. Cindy, I think it would be a real value for you to help Jeff with your ideas and finishes. And Jack you need to be in on the design since you are the one building it."

"I couldn't have said it better, little brother. So, my question Jeff, is how long do you need to have blueprints for my brother and I to see?"

"Well, we are going to need at least six months. There is a whole lot to design here. Every square inch had to be very well thought out, and not wasted. There is a whole lot of systems that we will need to design from scratch."

"Ok well We need to start construction no later than six to nine months from now, do whatever you need to get this done sooner if possible. Jack how long do you think it will take to build out?"

"It's going to take at least 24 solid months!"

"Wow I hoped it would be done sooner, but this is going to be a complicated build. Ok enough of this for the day."

"Dave, can you make sure are little surprise is ready?"

"Sure, thing boss!"

After a quick call he got back to me, "Yes, they are already for us."

"So, My Brother and I wanted to thank you for all coming out here today. And as you are planning on being here for a couple of days. We wanted to make you stay of comfortable as possible. So, I wanted you to know that I personally flew out a personal chef to cook for us all while you are here. I also have furniture you with your own rooms with your own bathrooms, and all the comforts of home. If you need anything at all. Please ask, Dave who hired a butler to take care of any of your personal needs. But please, let's go celebrate. Chef has prepared us all a wonderful seven course meal, I have a fully stocked bar, and wine cooler. I would like us all to celebrate tonight. Shall we head on up top side then.

As we sat down the waiter came around and took are drink orders, after a couple of drinks and appetizers everyone started letting lose and having an enjoyable time. After a few to many drinks, and an amazing dinner, we all then ended up retiring for the night, and then we headed back for our own rooms.

   I made myself comfortable, laid down on the bed, and started then watching TV. After about a half hour, there was a sudden unexpected knock on my door. I went to the door to see whom it was at my door. To my pleasant surprise, it was Cindy of all people, I was shocked when I had noticed that all she was now currently wearing at the moment was a very sexy see-through nighty, and a sexy warm smile, and holding a bottle of Jameson, that she had snatched from the bar. How could I turn her down, she was incredibly hot, ten years younger than me, and single just like me. I had no idea that she was attacked to me, but something had told me I wouldn't be getting much sleep tonight, if I were to invite her on in.

   "So, handsome you going to invite me in? It's a little cold standing out here like this. I was over in my room. Getting hot thinking about you, maybe it's the alcohol talking, but I don't really care. I know I didn't want to have to sleep all alone tonight! Knowing that you were over here, just across the hall from me. So, what do you say, can I stay the night with you?"

"If I were to say yes, then understand this, I will in all likelihood end up sleeping with you if you do."

As I had said this, her nighty suddenly mysteriously had suddenly dropped to the ground, and she was now standing in front of me, and completely naked, and smoking hot! Oh, she wasn't playing fair, not at all. I guess that I had my answer. I swept her up in my arms, shut the door with my right foot. She reached down and locked the door. We didn't want to be disturbed. And we began to kiss. I excitedly carried her now naked body back over to the bed. Which certainly led to a passionate night of very good sex, no unbelievable sex. We finally had managed to fall asleep somewhere around 2am. It had been a long time since I had physically been with a woman.

Then in the morning, there was a knock on the door around eight that breakfast was now ready. We woke up in each other's arms. I'm not sure that either of us knew what to say at the moment. Or if last night was just a mistake, or a one-time thing or not. Most of us have had this happen at least once in our adult life.

    Cindy acted first, thankfully breaking the awkwardness of the moment. She rolled over and kissed me. Then she pulled away just far enough, so I could look at her as she spoke to me. As she had talked to me. "Robert, all the alcohol I drank last night just gave me the courage to do what I have wanted to do for months now. Three months ago, when you first came to my office. I was so instantly attracted to you; I haven't been able to stop thinking about you ever since. Every time we have communicated with one another, I have gotten so excited, just to hear your voice. I looked you up and found out that your single. I needed you to understand how I feel about you. I don't want this to just be a booty call. So, if you don't feel the same about me, and you wanted to fire me from this project, because I crossed the line. I would completely understand, and I will pack up and leave this very morning. There won't be any hard feelings. I would be willing to quit the project if it means we can possibly have a chance at being together."

"I looked into her eyes and then I began to kiss her. Then I pulled her naked body close into me. She laid her head on my chest. Neither of us had to say anything more. Our actions had said it all. We laid naked there together a couple of minutes together. We were both in a little shock I'm sure, but we were both very happy with this recent outcome. We got up and then took a shower together. Then we talked about not letting anyone else know that we were now have hooked up, at least until after we all leave here after tomorrow. I let her use my robe. I slowly opened the door, looked to see if the coast was clear. And she snuck back safely to her own room which was just across the hall from me. Come to find out she had planned it that way. Then the plan was that we would meet up at breakfast. So, things wouldn't look suspicious to the others. I got dress and then headed down to the dining room. Everyone but Cindy was already there.

Cindy later came and joined the rest of us about twenty minutes later. She was positively glowing. I tried my best not to stare over at her, but I couldn't stop thinking about her. She was also having a challenging time. I haven't felt like this in a very, very long time. I know that I liked this unexpected feeling. Sitting directly across the table from me, she had begun innocently playing footsie with me. Oh, she really wasn't playing fair with me.

Trying to get my mind back on business through all that. The four of them, and Dave spent several hours down in the complex three dee mapping every square inch of the entire complex. That was where Dave's expertise and equipment had come in handy. I had to catch up on paperwork. The company didn't just run itself. Joe had joined the rest of them, acting in my behalf.

That night about an hour after everyone had retired to their own rooms, Cindy excitedly had come joined me once more. It was a long day not being able to not put my hands on her. We made up for it. Well one thing was for sure at this point, we were both certainly highly attracted to one another. We woke up early and snuck her back to her room before anyone could see what the two of us had been up to.

We all had one more day of work before we flew out the following morning. By the third night, I decided to go ahead and ask her to fly back with me, rather than going home just yet. I just had to spend more time with her, I had to figure out where this all was going between us. As we flew back to the airport, and everyone else caught their individual flights home, Cindy joined Joe and me on our private jet. Joe was rather surprised by this recent development. I never let him know ahead of time. He surprised me, and didn't say a single word, but he certainly had that little smirk of his. I knew I would hear about it later. Frankly, I didn't care. I at the moment was on cloud nine. I actually thinks that he was happy for me. Truth told; Cindy is the first woman that I had been with since sadly losing my wife to breast cancer three years ago. I hadn't gone on a single date. I guess I was finally ready to start dating again. He was relieved to see me with her. He sat upfront and gave the two of us are privacy. We talked the whole flight back. God, it felt good. I found her quite easy to talk to, and she was a great listener.

    Joe called his wife to tell her about me and Cindy, she was so happy for me. But the mother in her, just couldn't let things lay. She of course said that she was going to come and meet us at the hanger, once we had landed, so she could meet her in person for herself. Joe's wife was like a little sister to me. I have known her most of her life, so I could understand if she wanted to be a little protective towards me. She only meant well. I just didn't want anybody ruining this for me.

CHAPTER THREE:

"The Relationship"

With Cindy returned back with Joe and me. I realized I didn't have the time to actually being able to take a whole lot of time off. We were extremely busy at work. We had a lot of contracts to currently fill.

Being that Cindy was with me, Joe insisted that I go ahead and take at least couple days off, while she was in town. He would handle things at work for me. I think that he really did want to give me a chance at some measure of happiness for a change. Before Cindy I hadn't gone on a single date, since losing my wife Nancy. So, he knew that this was an awfully big deal to me. He knows how lonely I had been.

I brought Cindy back to my place. She actually had never been up to The San Juan islands before. I live on Whidbey Island. I just built a new house a couple of years ago. I had sold the house my wife and I had lived in a couple years earlier. I used to live in the Skagit valley. Close to where our business is located. My old house was too much of a constant painful reminded of her. I had just needed a fresh start.

   Cindy absolutely loved my house, and the view. My house sat in a quite area on the northeast part of the island. My view looked out at the water, and Fidalgo Island, and the mouth of the Skagit river, Mount Baker, and the Cascades. And I had stairs that led down the bluff, down directly onto the beach below. To be honest it was really nice having someone else staying in the house, other than just me. I really don't know why I had built such a large house just for me. I guess I had hoped that I would eventually marry and raise a family.

   It was extremely nice being able to spend one on one time alone with just Cindy and me. We spent a lot of time walking down along the beach. I also took her all over the island, showing her around. She absolutely loved it here. She cooked for me, and my comment to that is, my god is she a fantastic cook. We spent four wonderful days together. We took the time to try and get to know one another better. We surprisingly were really compatible. We had a lot of the same goals, and interests in life. We did broach the subject of marriage and kids. Our time together flew by much too quickly for me. I reluctantly drove her to the Skagit airport, under protest. I was having my pilot fly her home. Back down to Santa Barbra where she lives. It was a hard goodbye for us both. I drove from the airport back to the office.

    Today Joe and I were going to have a companywide meeting and let all our employees know about the company's expansion, and Joe taking over the day-to-day operation. But that means that we have to fill Joes old position. We strongly believe in promoting within the company.

    When I pulled up to the office, oddly everyone was glad to see me, they were all smiling at me oddly. I knew exactly why they were, Son of a bitch, Joe, or Catherine, Joes wife must has probably told everyone about Cindy. Catherine's are office manager. She can't keep a secret if her life had depended on it. And we are all like family here. So, I wouldn't put it past her, not for a second.

    There is one thing about Joes promotion, that was he was not getting, that was a new office, meaning mine. But that was no big deal, we had remodeled are offices just last year. Only the title on this door is going to be changing. Besides our offices were the same size, I had a slightly better view is all.

Before we made the big announcement, we wanted to meet with Walter. He was Joe and mine very first employee; he knows this company inside and out and has proved to have been a very loyal employee over the years. And he certainly deserves to be promoted. Question was would he want to come off the line and become a full-time pencil pusher. If he excepts the promotion, I'm going to have to train Joe, and then Joe is going to have to train Walter, and Walter will have to train his own replacement. So, there would be some pretty big changes, and temporary disruptions. But I really felt like this was all a very good thing. It was time. Change can be a good thing for a business, new ideas, and new blood. Companies can go stagnate without out making changes once and a while.

    "Walter, could you come up to my office."

    "Yes, boss you wanted to see me?"

    "Yes, please shut the door behind you. Please come in and sit down. So, you're probably wondering why I had called you here. So just so you know, Joe and I want to make some big changes around here. Things can't stay the way that they currently are. We are going to be currently expanding the company. That being said,

Joe and I talked, I'll just go ahead and come out with it, we want to go ahead and replace you. Its time! We need new blood in the line."

The look on Walter's face, thinking he was getting fire, and had no idea why! Maybe it was a little of the practical joker in me. I knew it was a little cruel. But I have known Walters for nearly twenty years. So, if he couldn't take a joke.

Walter, you have been with us a very long time. Hell, you were our very first employee. You have helped us make this company what it is today. So, we thought we would tell you first before anyone else. I thought that it would be better coming from the two of us. We are now starting a second company. We are going to be building high end nuclear fallout shelters. I'm going to run this new company and remain C.E.O of both companies. And Joe's becoming the president of both the companies. So, we will need a new vice president of the company. We want to promote you to the position of Vice president. There is no one at this company more qualified for this position then you. We need new blood in management. Of course, there will be some added perks with this promotion. Because of the position, we would like to put you on salary, So right now your making

$75,000. So, we will bump you up to $110,000, in addition, a 5% bonus based on your sales, and profits each quarter, and also, we want to give you an additional week of vacation, company credit card. New company vehicle. We need you to look the part.

Now I'm going to be honest with you, you're going to have to earn that raise. This position comes with a whole lot of hours, and a whole lot of stress, ask Joe about that." Joe just shook his head in agreement. "And you're going to have a whole lot of new responsibilities, including all the hiring, and firing for the entire company. You would be meeting with clients, and responsible for all the scheduling, of the manpower, and the jobs, and a whole lot of travel would be required. So, what do you say? Would you like to except the position, or would you like to stay in the position that you're currently at? No hard feelings if you want to just stay at your current job. We completely understand if you don't. But if you don't except the position, please understand that we would be forced to bring someone else in, and unfortunately they would become your new boss."

"Are you kidding me, absolutely yes, I want the promotion! Thanks guys!"

Joe spoke up, Walter you absolutely deserve this buddy! I'm really happy for you, Congratulations. You know what your first task as the new vice president of the company is going to be don't you? Well, its finding, and promoting, and training your replacement. So, we need you to get on this at once. And as soon as you have accomplished this. Joe will start training you for your new position. So, what do you say we go announce all this to the company." We have over fifty employees to share the news with.

It had been two long lonely weeks since Cindy and I had last seen one another. She had been busy with work. But we have been talking at least a couple of times a day, but it's just not the same thing. I'm not going to lie; I have been actually finding myself surprisingly missing her. She was coming up for another visit. She had the whole week off. The unfortunate thing for me, is that I completely swamped at work, so I couldn't break away for the entire week. But I was so excited to be getting to see her again. I picked her up at are hanger at the airport. My heart skipped a beat when I first saw her disembarking from the jet.

She had a pretty baby blue dress on. The week had gone by much too quickly. Before I had even known it, she was leaving once again. When I was taking her back to the airport. On the way, I really don't know what exactly had come over me, "Cindy, I know you have to travel for work and all. But I was thinking, and I know it's moving awfully quickly and all, for me to even be even suggesting this, but I really miss you when you're away. I would love to have you move in with me. Lord knows I have the room So, what do you say?"

She was silent for a moment, "Wow! So that's a big move Robert. I'm going to need some time to think about it. This is an awful big thing. Your right it is rather quick. She acted a bit standoffish after that. I just realized that I just may have screwed things up. I guess I was.

She boarded the jet; we kissed and said our goodbyes. I stood there and watched on as they took off. I was freaking out by this point. I was worried that I may have just scared her off, by moving too quickly. I was so mad at myself, what the hell was I even thinking anyways. I just went and scared her off.

Then as I was getting into my truck there was a new text, I just received from Cindy. I was very nervous. I opened it. "Darling I would love to move in together, I love it up here. I want to start a new life with you in it full time. I'll tell you what, I'll start packing when I get home. Then I wasn't sure if she had slipped, and meant to say it, but she ended the text with "I love you! I'll call you later this evening, and we can talk about all this then."

Not even thinking twice. I was so excited by her answer, I told her that was great news, and finished the text by saying, I love you too. Boy was that a big threshold that we both had just crossed. I was in completely uncharted territory here.

Her response back was a text full of hearts. I knew we were moving rather quickly. Most people think it was actually even perhaps crazy. But at least I knew that she wasn't after my money. Truth told; she actually comes from an ultra-wealthy family. So even though I am a multi-millionaire, her family is worth more than thirty billion dollars. She has a very large, several hundred-million-dollar trust fund, close to a billion dollars. But she doesn't ever touch it. She wants to make her own money. I really admire her for that.

CHAPTER FOUR:

"Design Is Completed"

I received a phone call from Jeff Hummel the other day. He shared with me that he has the designs for the bunker all completed. So, I was going to have him, and everyone else all fly out to our headquarters. I thought it would be best to meet here. We all agreed to meet on Wednesday at 11am. I had Cathine get them all rooms at the Majestic Hotel in Anacortes.

I thought that it was important that Cindy be there. We agreed to keep it professional during the meeting. Then we would tell everyone afterwards that we are now a couple. The fact that we were a couple had a really nice ring to it.

I had Catherine go pick up everyone at the airport. We were going to meet in the conference room.

"Well, I want to thank everyone for coming here today. Joe and I are very excited to finally see the blueprints. Jeff laid them out on the conference table. My god, they must have been at least three inches thick. To make it easier. We have an 85-inch monitor on the wall. Were Jeff could walk us through the entire faciality in 3-dimental. We supplied everyone VR googles.

    We all then turned our attention to the screen. We first started by walking in through the massive blast doors. He had plans for a nice warm inviting entry. Before anyone enters. They have to go through a small room to be blasted and sterilized. By blasted of sterilized air. Once the person had been treated, from there off to the left there is an elevator that went down from there. Then to the right is the control center to the entire complex. Everything can be controlled from this one room. Then I was surprised, but Jeff said that it would be needed. He had two jail cells added to his design. Its unpredictable just how people will begin to act after being locked up for so long. There was also a gun safe.

    The next ten floors below were for nothing but massive amount of storage for every kind of supplies that would possibly be needed, food related, and nonfood related supplies that we would possibly need over such a long period. Massive walk-in deep freezers. Everything would be automatically scanned with a bar code as it entered, or exited the freezer, or the storerooms, so that the inventory would always be updated instantaneously into the system.

Then the last four floors were entirely for equipment that was going to be needed to run all the systems which was including, water, water filtration, hot water, heat, power generation, oxygen production, air filtration, sewage treatment. Fire suppression, A blast oven, for waste disposal, including if needed to cremate someone's body, in case there are any deaths which could be very plausible in a five-year period. Several tesla massive house batteries. Massive generators, and large propane tanks to run the generators for backup if needed. And equipment to run everything electronic, and since everything was automated, and there was an internal internet, there was quite a bit of equipment that was needed. For safety, most systems were completely backed up with two separate system just in case something breaks down. Including having system back up. There was a small warehouse just for new parts, and electronics, enough to repair anything in the complex. At the lowest level there was the tunnel that connected to the next silo over. There was a blast door that would be controlled electronically. Without the proper security clearance owners wouldn't be able to enter these highly restricted areas. Dave said that the doors to the command silo, and food production silo, would be security doors to protect these critical area's just in case needed. All the systems, including thousands of miles of wiring, were fed through this access tunnels to connect everything together. Everything was monitored throughout the entire facility.

So, in the first silo this was entirely used for food growth. This silo has twenty stories. The first twelve stories were solely used to grow vegetables and fruits year-round. The vegetables would be grown hydroponically. Then things like potato's, berries, and fruits, and all manner of vegetables would be grown in large planters. The care for the plants, would be all automated, watered and fertilized. Then there would be L.E.D. grow lights that doesn't take a great deal of energy. Even the lighting would be automated. The oxygen that the plants then were producing will be captured, and not going to waste. The next eight stories would be to producing valuable protein. Several varieties of fish, muscles, and claims would be grown in large water tanks. Then chickens would be grown to be eaten, as well as for their egg production. Both the fish and chicken waste would then be gathered and then be turned into plant fertilizer to be used on the plants. And in the grains, we grew to feed the chicken, and fish. So, nothing would be wasted.

All floors would be constructed from concrete for noise. In silo number two was designed for entertainment purposes. The lowest floor there was a swimming pool, sauna, and a hot tub, and showers. With lounge chairs to lay around the pool. The ceiling and walls would electronically stimulate both the sky, and the sun.

The next floor up with thirty-foot ceilings was the sports multi court complex. For basketball, volleyball, pickle ball, even a climbing wall. Then the very next floor was a state-of-the-art gaming room. The next story had a koi pound with a waterfall. And around the pound, was a wide variety of all manors of tropical plants and trees. The ceilings were more than thirty feet tall to allow the trees to be able to grow tall. The ceiling was electronic to make it appear like a real sky, changing looks through the entire day. The room will be humid. There will also be birds, butterflies, and bees that pollinated all the tropical flowering plants, Walking path, and benches to sit on. The room will have artificial rain as well as wind. To make the experience of being in the room as realistic as humanly possible. And we had beehives to pollinated the fruit trees, and the vegetable plants. A secondary benefit was the honey that the hives produced.

   The next floor will have a small running track, and weightlifting room. The next story had a dance room, and yoga room. And showers.

   The next floor was a play area in case there are children that end up living there.

The next floor is a movie theater, with very comfortable recliners. And a very large screen more than two hundred inches, and state-of -the-art sound system. Just outside the theater there was a fully stoked concession stand. The library for viewing would include both more than a million movies, and Television shows to choose from. And as far as music there was thousands of songs to choose from.

   The next floor contains a library, craft rooms and a medical facility, and a card room. And rooms that could be used as classrooms if needed.

The last floor is a grand great room for entertaining, and fully stocked bar, and wine cellar, and a cigar room.

The next three silos had a total of forty-five condos. Fifteen in each silo. The buyers have a chance to choose the layout and finishes of the condo that they were buying.

It was at this point that Jeff had wrapped up his presentation to us. Joe spoke first, "Jeff, I really think you guys knocked this out of the park."

I then commented, I second what my brother had just said. I never imagined that we could make it this nice. I know this much, it's going to cost a fortune to build, but I imagine with all the added features, Cindy is going to be able to get quite a bit more per unit.

So, what do you think Cindy? Well first and foremost, Jeff I wanted to thank you, all the hours of craziness working along with you. I know I drove you utterly mad, but that being said, you beyond nailed it! So, Thank you for putting up with me.

If you all could give Joe and I a moment to go talk privately. The two of us got up and left the room, and then headed down to my office where we could talk freely. "Well Joe, what do you really think of all this, do you like it, and should we invest the kind of money that it's going to take to build such a place? It's going to require several million dollars, before we ever see a dime back in return."

"As your business partner, I say hell yes, let's do it."

"You sure about that? I mean, if this doesn't go well, how we plan, and the condos don't end up selling, it could end up bankrupting us."

"Absolutely! Without risk, then there is no reward. That's what you always say to me."

"So now you listen to me! Ok then let's do this!"

"We came back into the conference room. "Good news, Joe and I have decided to go ahead and move forward. So, Jack get the ball rolling, now that the design is finalized, you can develop a budget, and timeline for me. I want to get started on this project as soon as possible.

CHAPTER FIVE:

"Construction Begins"

So, it has been two months since giving the go ahead with the project, after the designs had been completed. And we finally got our needed permit. I was getting ready to fly out to the site for my first weekly inspection. While they had gotten started on the construction two weeks ago.

The rough overall budget for the build is now hovering around 100 million dollars. Trust me, I have had a whole lot of sleepless nights over that fact. But if everything goes as planned, then We should clear 40 to 45 million. Just depending how bad we end up going overbudget, and we will with a project like this. There is to many moving cogs for it not to. Joe and I were now in the big leagues. It was quite exciting, and nerve racking all at the same time.

On a more personal note, Cindy and I are doing really quite good these days. I am truly happy for the first time in years. Our relationship is growing stronger by the day. We have been together almost nine months now, it's hard to believe. And since she has moved in. She has completely redecorated the entire house on me. I really didn't mind. She has good taste. She just was trying to make it feel like home to her as well. Two months ago, we got a miniature Aussie, from a local reputable breeder. Cindy named him Kona. But having a new puppy is like having a little kid. I forgot just how much work they actually can be.

I haven't met her parents yet, but we have it planned to have them come up for a visit. They're going to be coming up on Saturday, for a three days. They are going to be staying at our place. That's when we were going to go ahead and tell them both about us being engaged. I know that I'm nervous about that. I am worried that they won't think that I'm good enough for their daughter, after all I would be marrying into old money. Even though I have been very successful with my company, with the kind of the money that they are worth, I make chump change comparatively.

I was a bit worried to be leaving Cindy behind, because she has been a bit under the weather the last couple of days. Unfortunately, I had to go. I had to be at the hanger at 4am. Cindy was still in bed sleeping as I was leaving. I gave her a kiss and left.

About an hour-in-half into my flight I was pouring over paperwork, when I received a text from Cindy, "Good morning poppa, I miss you already! The bed was cold without you here, lying next to me."

I thought that a rather strange text. I texted her back, I miss you too, poppa? Was it a sexual thing? I was confused.

Then a second text from her, "So you know I haven't been feeling well the last couple of days, well as it turns out, I'm not sick after all! It turns out that I'm actually pregnant! I just took a pregnancy test."

I couldn't believe it, I texted her back, "You're not joking, you're really pregnant?"

"Yes, honey I am. I am so excited!"

"I'm in shock, but I have never been truly happier! I love you so much. I have always wanted to be a daddy. I finally am going to be, wow, oh wow! Cindy, I love you so much."

Suddenly I couldn't focus on my work any longer. I was just so bloody excited! I just started out the window for a couple of minutes, then I gave her a call on my satellite phone. "Hello, Hi honey, I can't believe it! I'm so happy. So, what do you think about being pregnant?"

Well, I'm with the man I love. I have always wanted to have kids; I was starting to think that it was never going to ever happen. I can't wait to be your wife, and mother to your children. Thank you for giving me this amazing gift darling. You know it's funny I grew up filthy rich, but none of that ever meant anything to me. But being in love and being a mother is what I have always really wanted."

"Honey why are you crying? Are you ok?"

"Absolutely, I'm just crying because I have never been so happy before. And it has everything to do with you!"

I nearly started crying myself! I ended talked with her the rest of the flight. She was going to make an appointment with a doctor to get a checkup.

Things were quite active out at the site now that construction has begun. Also, the security around the property is now completely installed, fencing, cameras everywhere. But the defenses goes much further than that, there is sensers placed in the ground along the fence perimeter. When I pulled up to the gate to get in. There was now an armed guard. He checked my I.D. I also noticed that there was a guard on patrol.

The guard then said, "Welcome Mr. Hummel, it's a pleasure to meet you Sir. Dave and Jack are both expecting you Sir."

"Excuse me, what's your name young man?"

"Charlie Ross, Sir"

"Well Mr. Ross, you can call me Robert. It's a pleasure meeting you. I know if Dave had hired you, you must be top notched. I'm glad to have you aboard."

I was quite impressed with all of Dave's new security measures on site. As I pulled into the parking lot, I had noticed that the place was a beehive of activity. I could tell that there was a lot of cars now in the lot.

Jack had brought in a vast number of building supplies, and workers as well as equipment. Each worker had to pass an extensive background check to even be here. As well as sign a no discloser paper, agreeing to not talk about what is going on here. These same workers have constructed several top-secret government projects. They also had to agree to abide to a list of rules on their conduct while they worked and stayed here.

There were huge piles of concrete forms, rebar, and stacks of lumber. Then each subcontractor had at least one or several Connexus out on site. They were being used to store tools and supplies. I had to have two full time cooks. Because the workers stayed onsite for 21 day stretches, then 7 off. There was a whole lot of bunkers for them to stay. I wanted the workers to have something to do when they weren't working, they had a theater where they could watch movies, showers, laundry room, mess hall, and a small store to get supplies. A gathering tent where they could listen to music, play pool, have a drink, as well as access to Wi-Fi.

There was a huge crane now set up at the site. The kind you would see used on a skyscraper being built. Large enough that it could actually reach all the silos from directly above. All the silo doors were all wide open.

Dave came and met with me at my car, as I was parking, "Dave good morning, I'm quite pleased with all your new security measure now in place. I have to admit it was nice pulling up seeing all the new work going on here finally. I was relieved that this was all now finally happening."

Thinking to myself seeing all this, I would completely be lying to you if I didn't admit that I was freaking out about just how much money I am now spending. I was experiencing a bit of self-doubt. But I had to be confident in front of everyone.

"Thanks! Yes, I'm glad that they are now building the bunker."

"Dave before we head over to the bunker, you're actually the first to find out. I just found out on the flight out, that I was going to become a father! I just had to tell someone."

"Wow, well congratulations, you and Cindy must be so excited!"

"Oh, trust me beyond excited! So, hey what do you say we go over and check things out. I want to see what's going on inside.

So, Jack came over to meet us. "Good to see you, Robert. This is quite exciting, isn't it? They are currently starting at the bottom of each of the silos. Construction Elevator was installed in the command silo last week. Building out lowest floors first. Then once the concrete was poured. Any equipment, and heavy materials would be then craned down, before beginning the floor directly above. What do you say that we go down and take a look for ourselves?"

I responded back, absolutely! Oh, by the way Jack, I have some exciting news to share with you! On the flight out, I found out that I am going to be a father!"

"Wow congratulation, that's fantastic news! Later we should have a drink to celebrate."

"Robert why don't we go ahead and go inside. Here's a hard hat for you. You will need to wear this. I would like to show you a couple things. Just as we were about to head inside, a concrete truck rolled up to the site. The crane lifted the massive bucket over to the back of the concrete truck. Once the bucket was full. The crane was then lowered the concrete down two hundred feet down into the command silo. The slab for the first floor was going to take 130 yards. The concrete slab was being poured eight inches thick. The new hydro wells were already drilled and installed. This slab would be housing a whole lot of very large equipment.

I stayed and watched the entire pour. It took thirteen concrete trucks to complete the pour. While one crew was pouring the concrete slab. A second crew was working over on the next silo over, prepping for the new slab. For a second pour in two days. Then the third silo over, heating ducts, and conduit for fiber optics, electrical, and plumbing pipes. In addition, the pool and hot tub was being formed up. And was going to be poured at the same time. Expect they would use shotcrete on the pool and sauna.

   By Jack having so many crews working, working in different areas, the job would be speed up considerable. He had more than a hundred people working on the complex at any one time. Then once the slab was poured and cured for a week, then the next story would then be started. All the shoring would be built off the story below. Then crews would add the plumbing pipes, conduit for electrical and fiber optics, and heat ducts. Then a mess load of rebar. Forming up the elevator shaft. Once that story had been poured and had cured. The forms would be pulled. And then framers, plumbers, and electricians, and heating contractors would be then brought in and would be brought in and start the build out on that story internal walls and mechanical rough in.

   I was quite impressed with the progress that they had been made in just two weeks. Later Jack and I when back up to the office. I spent a couple hours going over things with Jack. Then I spent about an hour with Dave, my assistant on this project. Not only is he in charge of keeping this site secure. But he overseer's things in my absent. One of the things that he wanted to show me is this week, that He had sunk all the camera's above, and below ground tied to my phone. So now I could check up on the site at any time.

   I was planning on coming out to the site once a week, and when I wasn't able to be here, I could have conference calls, or facetime. I expected to constant be kept in the loop. I desired to be very hands on all the way thru. Especially on the cost.

   I wrapped things up. Then Jack, Dave and I went and had a drink to celebrate, then I drove back to the airport. Then my pilot flew me home. I had been so busy all day, that I forgot to even tell Joe the exciting news yet! I called him on the flight back. He was so happy for me.

I landed about 7pm. It had been a very long exciting day. I couldn't wait to get home to Cindy. I was so excited to see her. We had some celebrating to do.

CHAPTER SIX:

"Future In-Laws"

    Cindy spent all day Thursday cleaning the house. Though she could afford to have a housekeeper. She has always preferred to do it herself. Cindy didn't like all the trappings of being super rich. Her parents were arriving at the airport at 9am in the morning. I was so bloody nervous about meeting them. We left about 8 to go pick them up from the airport. On the way there Cindy made me promise her to not say anything about the baby, or the engagement just yet. She thought over dinner tonight would be a good time to break the news to them. She wanted to give her parents the day to get to know me first. Before just springing it on them so suddenly. I wondered what she had meant by that. Then I wondered if I should be nervous or not. Because I was, her family comes from old money. So, I worried that they would think that I wasn't good enough for their daughter. Or perhaps I was after their money. I was suddenly having a whole lot of self-doubt that I wasn't going to measure up for them.

I had my pilot fly them out, maybe I thought that it was me trying to impress them just a little. Cindy was as well because she was all onboard with it. I could tell that she was as nervous as me, maybe even more so, she's daddy's little girl, his only daughter. And she wasn't sure how her parents were going to take the big news. One thing that might bowed in her favor, was that her older brother isn't married, or have any kids, and she knew that her parents wanted to be grandparents in the worst way. She knew this fact because they mention it to her all the time.

As soon as they got off the jet, Cindy immediately ran over and gave her parents a great big warm welcoming hug. They hugged her right back. I slowly walked over towards them. Not knowing how this was going to end up going.

Her dad released his hug from his daughter, and then glanced over at me, as I was now approaching them, "So this must be the man that has managed to capture me daughter's heart. I have to tell you young man, over the last nine months, I'll be honest with you, I have never seen her so happy before this. She's constantly talks about you, so I thought it was hide time that I come and meet you in person for myself. Meet you for myself."

"Daddy you be nice to my man! I don't want you scaring him off, he's a keeper. So, you better like him."

I reached my hand out, "It's a pleasure to meet you Sir, And may I just say you have quite a daughter. Hey why don't I go get your luggage, my pilot gave me a hand. I loaded their luggage up, and then we drove home.

On the way back, "So, Robert, I liked you Lear Jet that's the new gulf stream two, isn't it?"

"Yes, Sir, we bought it new last year."

"I was thinking about getting a new one, it's quite comfortable."

I must admit that made me feel good that I had at least impressed him a little. Her parents had never been up to the San Juans before. Luckily, there wasn't a cloud present in the sky. They seem to love it; They especially loved the drive over the deception pass bridge. I went ahead and parked in the parking lot on the Whidbey island side, so we could get out and walk out on the bridge and enjoy the amazing view in person. Cindy's mom took lots of pictures.

As we pulled up to the house, they were pleasantly surprised, not expecting me to have such a nice place. Maybe not as big and as fancy as theirs, but I couldn't compete with their old money. But my house was over seven thousand square feet. Fourteen hundred square feet of covered deck, and a large deep six car garage. And right on the water, bet I have a better view, then they have. I have five acres.

I didn't bother pulling into the garage. I wanted to make sure that they came in thru the front day. I wanted to impress them some. As you walk into the house, through the oversized front door. The great room is twenty-nine feet tall at the peak, with exposed wood beam trusses, the ceiling was cedar tongue and groove. In the far corner is a real massive stone fireplace that goes all the way to the ceiling. And the back is all glass windows, with oversized sliders, that open out onto a massive, covered deck with a hot tub and a fire pit. And a kitchenet with a barbecue. On the other side of the great room, is a fully stocked bar, and behind that, an eleven hundred bottle wine cellar.

As I was opening the front door, Little Kona snuck by me, and then excitedly came running up to great us all. "Who's this cute little fellow?"

"Mom, that's Kona. Isn't he just the cutest. Robert bought him for my birthday. Oh, he is so smart, wait till I show you all his tricks."

"Oh, he's absolutely adorable!"

Thank god, her parents had loved the place. It was such amazing evening out that we decided that we would eat out on the deck and enjoy the commanding view. Cindy had spent the afternoon cooking dinner for us. Doris had been helping her. It gave them a chance to checkup, meanwhile Frank and I sat out on the deck drinking scotch, and smoking cigars. And getting to know one another. He was relieved that I was a Republican. He asked me a whole lot of questions about my business. He actually appeared to be quite interested in what I did for a living. He didn't realize that my company was so large. And that we build are shelter all over the world. Or that are company was the larger of its type in the world.

"Say Robert, when are you going to that project again?"

"Next Friday! Why do you ask?"

"Well, I was thinking if you don't mind, I would love to go with you. I find it very fascinated what you are building. So, I went to my office, and I went and got my laptop, so I could show him the blueprints. He was completely blown away.

About an hour later, Doris came out, "I hope you boys are hungry? Because dinner is now ready."

As we were sitting down, I asked hey would you both like some wine?"

"Sure!"

"I was thinking perhaps a nice cab. Cindy and got this bottle when we went to Walla Walla. As I said this, I realized my mistake, I forgot that Cindy couldn't drink." I thought shit!

"That would be great Robert! I did my best to play it off."

I started pouring the wine, I skipped pouring any for Cindy. Her Dad saw that she wasn't drinking. He knew that she loves wine. So, he thought that was odd.

"Cindy, aren't you going to join us sweetheart?"

"No, daddy, I have cut back. I'm just having water, but hey you please go ahead and enjoy yourself."

That's when Cindy gave me that look, I knew what the look was for. It was now, or never. Cindy then nervously had said, "Daddy, and Mom, I am so happy that you both came up for a visit. I've missed you both so much. But there is another reason why I had invited you here this weekend. You see Robert and I are very happy together. I have never felt like this for anyone. And well I think that you should both probably know that Robert asked me to marry him, and I of course said yes! I had wanted to share the news with you both in person. I wanted you to meet Robert before I had told you."

Doris was the first to speak up, I thought oh boy here it comes,

"Oh, that's wonderful news darling! Congratulations to the both of you, Well then, I guess we have a wedding to plan. Oh, I'm so excited!"

Her dad then abruptly stood up, and came over to me, he looked right directly at me. "I can see how happy you have made my baby girl. I can see that you are a good man, and a self-made person. That I can truly respect. So, I give you both my blessing!" Cindy came over and gave her dad a hug. Both her parents appeared to be pleased by the unexpected news.

We all sat back down, Mom dad, wait before you start eating, there is something else that I need to share with you both. Mom dad the reason I'm not drinking, is that I'm actually pregnant!"

Her father this brave stoic man, started to cry, when he heard the news. "Daddy, are you mad at me?"

"Baby why would you think that I'm mad at you, I am just so happy! This is the best possible news! Your, mom and I are finally going to be grandparents, family is everything! I thought between your brother and you that we were never going to become grandparents!"

"Daddy, I did want you to know, that we aren't getting married because I had gotten pregnant. No in fact Robert had asked me to marry him three weeks before we even knew I was pregnant."

Her dad, commented, "Honey I can see that you have a real standup guy!"

"Cindy, I couldn't be happier about all this. How far along are you?"

"I saw my doctor the other day, she said that I'm eight weeks. She said everything looks good, she put me on prenatal vitamin."

Doris had a huge smile on her face, "I can't believe my baby is now going to have a baby of her own." Then she started to ball!

I then tried to lighten the mood a little, What do you say if we go ahead and eat this wonderful food that you both worked so hard making us."

Cindy piped in, "I second that."

But than her dad had said, "You two don't have any more big surprises for us do you? I don't know how much more excitement that your mom or me could take in just one day?"

"No Daddy, that's it!"

We all had started laughing.

I was very relieved that I had received Cindy's parents seal of approval. The following day I thought it would be fun if we took my boat out and took her parents up to San Juan island. It's about an hour-in-half boat ride out to the island, from the marina. But it's a beautiful route. Taking us between several islands like Shaw and Lopez, and Orcas island. The plan was to first go into Friday Harbor. Do a little site seeing, grab a bit, then take them to the other side of the island. Take a look at all the large mega yachts in the marina, at Roche harbor. Then we will sail down the west side of the island, then home going around the south end of San Juan Island, along the south end of Lopez island. Then back over to Whidbey island, and then back thru Deception Pass, and then back around to the east side of the island and back into Cornet bay, were I moored my boat.

We left the dock about 9 am. Once I got the boat passed deception pass. Some very strong currents as the tide was going in. I asked Mr. Hoskins if he wanted to pilot the boat. He was excited but surprisingly had never actually done that before. I was rather surprised by this. So, I gave him the crash course. He was a quick study. Turns out he was in hog heaven. He absolutely loved it. Cindy and Doris spent the whole time taking about the wedding, and the baby. I just let them be.

We got back to the marina around 4pm. We took her folks out to Frasier's in Oak Harbor for dinner. The next morning over breakfast, both Cindy and I got a huge shock of our own. It was our turn to be surprised. "Robert, Cindy, Doris, and I are so excited to have you marry our daughter. I have never seen her this happy before, its clearly all because of you. That's all I have ever wanted for her. And of course, that fact that we are going to have a grandchild on the way, wow. We are so excited by this news.

   I can understand why my daughter wanted to move up here; as it turns out, we love it up here as well. My wife and I have traveled all over the world, but by far, this place is one of the most beautiful places we have ever been. So that all being said, and if it would be ok with you both, we would like to be closer to the both of you, and our new grandchild. We would like to build a house here on the island, so we have a place to stay when we come up for a visit. So, we could stay for a longer period, and not have to impose on you two. And be able to baby sit our grandchild. Of course, we wouldn't be able to live up here full time. But we wouldn't even consider such a move as this, if you both aren't good with it."

    Both Cindy and I looked at one another, we could see how important this was to her parents, and I knew Cindy would love having family nearby, like I have. I really didn't have a problem with it. "That is an amazing idea, in fact I know a piece of property for sale just about a half a mile down the road from here. With the exact same view as mine. I'll tell you what, let's walk down after breakfast and take a look at it. See what you both think of it. I think it would be perfect for you.

    They ended up loving it, called the real estate agent and put an all-cash offer in on the lot the same day. Of course, to insure they got their hands on the lot they offered a hundred thousand over the asking price, and they would do a quick close. I then gave them the number to the contractor that I had used to build my house. The real estate agent called back an hour later saying that their offer was accepted. Afterwards Cindy and I drove her folks back to the airport.

    After dropping them off, Cindy was so happy! "Oh my god Robert, they absolutely loved you, I was so bloody worried that they wouldn't. They have never liked anyone that I have ever dated. I couldn't believe that they are so happy for us. To be honest, I didn't think it was going to go so well.

Are you sure your good with them just living down the road from us?"

"I thinks it's a great idea! You'll have family nearby, and we will have a built-in babysitters. I am so relieved that they liked me and gave us their blessing. To be honest, your parents are pretty cool! Not what I had expected at all. To be honest, I was extremely worried they weren't going to like me. Especially since I don't come from money.

CHAPTER SEVEN

"Job site Visit!"

I met up with Cindy's father Frank at the Wichita airport around nine am. He had flown in on his personal jet. We then rented a car, and then we drove out to the sight. We rolled up to the gate passed through security. We then met up with Dave. "Dave I would like to introduce you to Frank, this is Cindy's father. He wanted to come out and see our little project here. Frank, Dave is my assistant here.

Frank reached and shock Dave's hands. Dave then said, "Nice to meet you Sir. You have quite a daughter. So, why don't I go ahead and give you a tour of the place."

I spoke up, "That would be great! So, where's jack hiding out at the moment?"

"Oh, he's down in silo number three. I'll go ahead and let him know that you're now here."

"Dave, I'll tell you what, why don't you go ahead and tell him to go ahead and stay there, we'll catch up with him in a little later."

Dave went and got us both hard hats. Then we walked over to silo #1 and looked down. Frank was surprised just how far down it really was all the way down to the bottom. Then we headed over to the command silo. I told him what the plans were for this silo. I pulled up the plans of the command silo, so I could show him what we were now looking at. We then took the construction elevator all the way down to the bottom.

Since I was here last, this slab had cured, and the large pieces of equipment was now being installed, and the next story above was at the beginning stages of being formed up.

"What do you think Frank? It's going to be quite impressive, isn't it?"

"This place is going to be absolutely massive. I knew it was going to be big. But I really had no idea. It's going to be like a city underground. But all self-contained. How long of period do you think people could hold up for?"

"We figure that upwards of up to seventy- five people could comfortably hold up for upwards of five years.

We then headed on over to silo #1 they had poured the slab that they were working on last week, when I had been here on my last visit. And prepping for the next story above. The next silo ground floor was taking a lot longer, because they are still working on forming the pool, and the hot tub areas.

   Then the last three silos, the living quarters they were currently being forming up the bottom floors in each of the silos, as well as the elevator shafts. We had spent about two hours down below walking through the site. Then Frank and I headed back up top side with Jack, and then the three of us back up to the office. Then Jack and I met in his office, and went over the schedule, and went over the budge, and looked at expenses. When it came to this stuff, I'm very hands on. I wanted to know how every single cent was being spent. I had way too much on the line not to.

   After are meeting had concluded, "Frank would you like to go to the mess hall, and grab a bit? We both have a flight to take. And The chef is quite good. I know that I'm starving!"

   "Sure, why not!"

Over lunch, Frank mentioned how impressed he was with my project, so what he said next surprised me a little! "Robert, I want to purchase one of the condos. Since you and Cindy are going to have one, I figure why not, just in case, one never knows. I'm looking at it as an insurance policy of sorts. God forbid something bad were to happen, I would want to be with my family, if the time should ever arise. I'll go ahead and write you a check now for my deposit, how much should I make it for?"

"Our you sure about this Frank? You really don't have too."

"Absolutely, so how much do you need for a deposit?"

"two point five million!"

He didn't even fletch at the amount. He then handed me over the check, "Really, Ok I'll go ahead and reverse the condo right above ours! You can work with Cindy on your layout, and design. Well congratulations I guess are in order!"

"Speaking of my daughter, how's see feeling?"

"Oh, she has been getting really bad morning sickness. I told her she should take a little time off.

I was actually surprised when she had agreed with me. She works so hard. She wanted to start planning for the wedding. She wants to focus on being a wife and mother for a while. I told her that I would support her, whatever she decides to do."

"Oh, good for her! While you were in your meeting, my wife had called me. And as it turns out, She's flying back out to your place for a couple of days, so her and Cindy could start the wedding planning. I guess that its time that I need to warn you. Knowing my wife, and I know my wife, she is going to go completely way overboard with the wedding. It's going to cost me a fortune, that much I assure you. And I promise you this much, neither you nor I will have no say in any of it. So, my best advice for you at this point, just go along with it. It will be much easier on you own sanity. Robert now that you're marrying my daughter, I would like to give you a small piece of advice if I may. I do love my daughter, but she can be very stubborn when she wants to be, she's just like her mother in that regards. So just going into your marriage knowing you will never ever win an argument. So just learn this saying, Here practice this sentence with me, "sorry honey, your absolutely right!" "It's worked quite well for me over the years."

We both started laughing! I knew he was absolutely right. "Boy are you right, Cindy can be quite stubborn at times.

After lunch we both headed back to the airport. Frank wasn't heading directly home. He actually was flying to Chicago for a board meeting. I on the other hand flew home. Come to find out that Frank sat on the Board of eleven fortune 500 companies. I was quite impressed.

CHAPTER EIGHT:

"The Big Day!"

The big day was rapidly approaching quickly. And Cindy's parents were sparing absolutely no expenses, to throw us a mega wedding. They must have spent a couple million dollars easily, which blows me away that one has that kind of money. I didn't want a big wedding, but it was Cindy's first, and well let's face it, Cindy's parents were stinking filthy rich. So, they naturally had to show off to all their rich friends. Some of the richest, and very famous people were invited to the wedding. People I would have never dreamt of ever meeting. Let alone coming to my wedding.

We were getting married at the four seasons resort on the big island. It's the resort that all the rich stay at when they come to the Big island. Her parents I couldn't believe rented the entire resort out for five entire days and nights. I could only imagine what that alone must have cost them to do so. Plus added security was being brought in. Because there was going to be a lot of very rich powerful people that would be attending our wedding. And because of who Cindy's family was, there would be reporters, and photographers who would have loved to get pictures of are event. But security was ordered to keep them out, and away from us.

I just wanted a simple wedding, but I quickly discovered that I had no say in any of it whatsoever, other than I was invited to the wedding. Not when you're marrying into a family that is the tenth richest family in the United States. I wish my parents could have come, but my parents aren't still alive. So, the only family I could invite, was my brother Joe, and his family, and a couple of cousins, and an aunt on my mom's side. I also invited about forty of my close friends. The other three hundred people coming, were all from Cindy's side. I was going to surely feel like a duck out of water, I'm sure. I had no idea how to act proper around people this stinking rich. I was worried that they all would look down on me, because of the fact that I hadn't come from money, like them.

We flew over to the big island on Wednesday, and the wedding was going to be on Saturday. After landing, the resort had sent a limo to pick us up at the airport. Then Cindy and I were taken to the Honeymoon bungalow, and Joe and his family to their bungalow. We were going to get unpacked, and situated, and then later, we were all going to be meeting down at the pool. In an hour. None of the guest were going to start to arrive until tomorrow afternoon. So, until then the whole resort was all our playground. And Cindy's parents will be here in time to have dinner with us tonight.

So, we had some time to just try and relax, be ourselves. We all headed down to the beach. The resort was catering to our every need. They served us only the best food, and liquor. No expense was being spared. The strangest part. We were the only ones at the resort. The ocean water was so warm, clear and an amazing blue color. The beach was absolutely amazing. The sand was perfect golden brown, no rocks. And there was green turtles sunbathing right there on the beach. They were quite large. We were told that we must stay twenty feet away from them at all times, they are a protected species in the state.

Cindy looked so beautiful, in her swimming suite. She's just starting to, really now show. She's now five months pregnant. To be honest, I found it to be really sexy look on her. Her boobs were getting really large. She had been working out, so she has been keeping in pretty good shape during her pregnancy.

We all had a fantastic time. It really felt good to just unwind, and truly relax. I have been working so hard lately. So, a little time off, away from work was going to be good. I have been so stressed out lately. My project was taking a real toll on me.

Tomorrow night after the rest of our guest have arrived. They are going to throw us a huge Luau for are rehearsal dinner. And at the dinner come to find out that Taylor Swift is going to actually be performing for us. As it turns out Cindy and her are great friends, they grew up together. Small world right. Truth told; I really didn't care for her music. We had her out to the house once.

Our ceremony was going to be held right there on the beach. We were going to be having a Hawaiian minister conducting are wedding. Luckily, I didn't have to wear a tuxedo. Cindy wanted me to wear a nice pair of shorts, and a nice black dress shirt. She didn't want it to be traditional wedding thankfully. At least her and her mom had listened to me on that much.

So, the Luau was starting at 7pm and our dress rehearsal was going to be at 5pm. Joe and I went down to the beach. Frank pulled Joe and I aside. "Joe, I wanted to take a moment to tell you that, it isn't just Robert marrying into the family, but that Joe as you being Robert's brother, business partner, and best friend, You are also going to be family to me. And as a token of gratitude, I wanted to give you both a pre-wedding gift. Go ahead and please open them up." He had Rolex's customed made for us, so they were truly one of a kind.

Joe spoke up, Thanks Frank, that means a lot. This watch is amazing! They were probably worth about three hundred thousand a piece, easily."

I could tell that Joe was a little chocked up. I could tell that gesture had meant a lot to him. Especially since we lost our own father. That gesture also meant a lot to me.

The wedding coordinator who was also hired to oversee everything over the three days while the guest were staying here. She was working with the events planner from the Four Seasons, and a whole lot of staff to make sure that this all went off without a single hitch. She told Joe my best man, and the Maiden of honor walked down the aisle after me. Taylor Swift was one of Cindy's brides' maids. Then each one of the wedding party afterwards.

Then we all stood there, then the flower girl, and the ring barrier walked together down the aisle. Then finally the orchestra that they flew in especially for the wedding. Then I turned around to watch my bride, and her father now walking towards me. It was at this moment that it had started really hitting me just a little. That this shit was now getting real. I really couldn't believe that tomorrow was going to be the big day.

I was relieved to find out that the rehearsal was now over. And they were ready to start the luau. All are guest were starting to arrive and being seated. They had Cindy and I sitting at the wedding party table. Everything was the best of the best, There were flowers everywhere.

The drink being served was Mia Tia's, they were really good, and unexpectedly strong. The Rum used in the drink was distilled on Kawaii made from pure sugar cane grown on Kawaii.

All our guest were comfortably now sitting, talking amongst themselves, and enjoying themselves, then Frank went up on stage to say a few words to all the guest. "Aloha everyone, I wanted to thank everyone here for coming, and celebrating this wonderful event with my family. I sincerely hope that you all truly enjoy yourselves. I am very pleased that you're all flown to see my baby girl getting married. Being a father, there is no greater joy, then to see your baby girl grow up into an amazing woman. Now she's getting married and starting a family of her own, there is truly no greater joy then this. Now let's be honest when you daughter tells you that she is getting married. As a father its natural to wonder if the guy that she wants to marry is worthy enough to marry your baby girl. So, in the case of My further son-in-law, well I would like to say that she hit the jackpot with him. I am proud to welcome Robert into the family. Robert, Cindy both of you would you please stand up please." We both stood up, and everyone began to cheering for us! All we could do, is just politely smile, and wave to everyone.

"Ok I think you all have heard enough of my rants; tonight, let's all celebrate! While you are at the resort, if you need anything at all, the staff is here to take care of you. The entire resort is reversed for us. So please all try and enjoy yourselves, eat, drink, and be, marry! I want to thank you for all coming." Frank came back over and joined us once more at the table. Everyone began to cheer!

They started taking the pig out of the ground, wear it has been cooking for the last 24 hours in the Hawaiian way. The staff putting this all on was Hawaiian and dressed just like the ancient Hawaiians would have done it. And everyone started getting up to get their food. I think my favorite food item to eat of this whole meal, were these amazing homemade coconut rolls. I don't know how many Joe and I had eaten of those. But let's just say it was much more than two.

Then the entertainment had started up after it was dark. First as a surprise to everyone. Taylor Swift went up on stage, then she grabbed the mic and began to speak, "Hello everyone, I wanted to surprise Cindy, she is one of my best friends, this is a gift for you, sweety! I am so happy for you both, Robert you better take good care of her." and she then began to preform for the next hour. She put on quite a little show. Then she introduced the performers. They put on one hell of a great show as well. I was called up on stage to dance like a true Hawaiian, being the groom. It was a good thing that I had had a couple of drinks beforehand. I just went with it, let loose, and had some fun.

So, Cindy wanted to be old fashion, and not sleep in the same bed as me tonight, or for that matter have sex. In fact, when I said good night to her, I was going to see her again, until the actual wedding tomorrow. I was going to walk Cindy back to the honeymoon bungalow. She had invited her girlfriends over to have a little get together. Me on the other hand, I was planning on meeting up with the guys back down at the bar. This was a really cool place. Tekke lights lined the walk path. The walk path was lined with bungalows, and then behind the bungalows, and a row of coconut trees, and behind that was hotel rooms. Cindy and I held hands on the way back. A few of people that Cindy knew spotted the two of us, and told us both congratulation, and what a cute couple we are.

"Robert, I wanted you to know how excited I am to be marrying you, and finally becoming a mother to your child. I have absolutely no regrets whatsoever about all this. I am so excited to be to marrying you tomorrow. Robert you should know this is all that I have ever wanted."

"Honey, I want you to know I fell the very same way. I'm certainly going to miss you lying next to me tonight."

"Hey, I know your meeting the guys down at the bar. Why don't you go have some fun, let loose a little, but just please promise to not drink too much. I need you sober enough, and not hungover at the wedding, I love you; I'll see you tomorrow! You better save your energy for our wedding night. I just think that you might get lucky. Honey, I have to go lay down, I'm kind of tired. Oh shit! I forgot the girls were coming over."

I gave her a big hug, and a kiss, and said try to have some fun! good night sweetheart. I then went to go join up with the guys down at the bar, It looked like a lot of are guest had the very same idea as us, to head to the bar. They had a band playing. They sounded pretty good. I headed down to the bar which was located right there on the beach. After a couple of drinks, Frank came up to me, so Robert, there is something you should probably learn about the ultra-rich, and parties and weddings. They are an excellent time and place for conducting business deals. I just wanted you to know that I have done just that. As my new future son-in-law. I wanted you to know that I wanted to help you and Joe out with selling your condo's. I have told all my like-minded very rich friends about your project. Many of them expressed quite a bit of interest, and verbally told me that they had wanting in. Because how they are. I wanted to be sure that I got you top dollar for the condos. You see with the ultra-rich. It's about having something that the others don't have and being the first to have it, it's a competition amongst them. I have set up a meeting the week you get back from your honeymoon. There is a good chance you will not only sell out, but I predict a bidding war will be occurring. I hope you don't think I'm overstepping here, but you're going to be family, and family should help family. And I know that you were counting on Cindy to sell the units out. But now that she's not. I know you have a lot of pressure on you to get the condos sold. I just wanted to help you is all. You certainly have enough on your plate at the moment. I wanted to help lighten your burden a little."

"Thank you, Sir, that's great news! I really appreciate it."

We all ended up closing down the bar. I hadn't been this drunk in a very long time, maybe a good decade or more. I don't even know how exactly I had made it back to my bungalow. I had really tied one on. The next thing that I remember is a loud knocking on the door. I grudgingly looked at the clock to see what time it was. It was after 11am. Then I realized that this was actually the big day. I also discovered my head was now absolutely pounding. All my family and friends were all planning on meeting up for brunch. At noon. I took some aspirin and drank a whole bottle of water. Oh yay, I also threw up. I actually felt a little better after that. Used some mouth wash.

    The wedding was at 5:00. Right before the sun goes down. Oh, did I wake up hung over, absolutely. But I also woke up really surprisingly fucking nervous. The reality was now really starting to now set in hard. I was so unexpectedly nervous that I actually didn't end up eating anything at brunch. I just drank a Bloody Mary to help with the hair of the dog. After brunch, I left all my mates behind, and then took a stroll down the beach by myself. I had to clear my head a little. While I was walking down on the beach, I called Cindy, she never said I couldn't call her. She was hanging with the girls, and doing her makeup, and hair. We had a really good talk. She made me fell a whole lot better. She can have a real calming effect on me. Something that I really appreciate her for.

The guys and I met up at the pool. Smoked cigars and drank some very special scotch. It was weird I was both very nervous, and very excited all at the same time. We all headed back to my bungalow, to start getting ready. I have a small token of my love sent over to Cindy. I sent a locket necklace with a picture of the two of us. And a dozen bird of paradise flowers, her favorite. And a sweet note that I wrote a couple of days ago. It was a little sappy, but she likes sappy. I just hoped that she hadn't read it aloud.

The guest started arriving at the wedding venue. The ushers started seating everyone. Once everyone was seated. Beth the wedding coordinator had the orchestra start playing the music. Then I walked by myself towards the minister. Everyone watched me, as I had walked by them. Then the Wedding party started walking down the aisle towards me, and the minister. I just stood nervously there in the sand, bare foot. With everyone now in position. My nerves really started now setting in. I was nervously standing there for what had seemed like hours, but in reality, was only a couple of minutes. The sun was quite warm. I was growing more nervous by the second. I wasn't sure that I could actually go through with this suddenly, but then the wedding march suddenly had started playing. I knew exactly what that meant. I slowly turned around and saw Cindy and her father now coming down the aisle towards me. She looked beyond beautiful. I felt like the luckiest man in the world at that very moment. And I suddenly realized that I desired to be nowhere else, but right here. I took a deep breath, and then smiled.

    I was so nervous; I could tell that Cindy was as nervous as me. And not to mention it was really hot out. One cool thing, a large green turtle had ended up strolling out of the water. And was relaxing only about twenty-five feet from us. The minister had Cindy and I repeat things back in Hawaiian, I had no idea what exactly we had just said, or if I had even pronounced it correctly. Then before I knew it, the minister was pronouncing that Cindy and I were now husband and wife. I gave my new bride a kiss. Then the two of us began walking down the aisle now united. Suddenly I was no longer nervous. I felt like a heavy load had been lifted off of me. We headed back to the bungalow so Cindy could change out of her wedding dress, and into something more comfortable, and a whole lot sexy. Then we would go meet everyone at are wedding dinner.

   The wedding dinner was truly amazing. And watching my wife dance with her father was the best. The evening had flown by. At the end of the evening, my wife and I headed back to the bungalow. After all it was my wedding night. The next morning all are guest met up for breakfast, before flying back home. Everyone was flying out today, except for Cindy and I, we were going to be staying on at the resort for the next week to celebrate our honeymoon. And go explore the island a little while we were here, let loose, and just have some fun. Make some new memories.

CHAPTER NINE:

"The Big Sell Out"

So, the honeymoon was certainly great. But business is business, Just three days after Cindy and I had gotten back from our honeymoon. We both had ended up flying out to the jobsite. We had been preparing for the big open house. Joe flew out two days ago to get things all ready. Cindy wanted to come with me. She also had her entire team go out the same time as Joe. There was a whole lot riding on this meeting tomorrow. We had 51 condos to sell, and the clients that would be coming, all had the kind of money to write some very big checks without thinking twice about doing so. We had to make sure that they were impressed. We had really hoped to sell them all out, at this single open house. Cindy and I had been working on pricing. In the end, we ended up deciding that because of the clientele that we were currently going to be going after, we have decided to raise the asking price from 4 million up to 5 million per unit. I realized working with Cindy, that she really knows what she is doing. I was excited to have her onboard. I knew that by the end of tomorrow. There could be a very good chance. That We are going to be a whole lot richer than when I woke up this morning. More money than I have ever made in my entire life. And the financial burden of building this place would finally be lifted. We could pay off all our debt. And I could sleep at night again.

Once we had arrived at the site. Cindy immediately met up with her entire team. Meanwhile I met with Joe, Dave, and jack. We took our own tour. Cindy and her team had been arranging everything. They had arranged for three helicopters to fly the clients out from the airport. And one of Cindy's team members would be there to meet and greet clients as they had arrived at the airport. Cindy had arranged an entire area at the airport for all the Lear jets to be able to park on the tarmac. And for the helicopters to fly clients in and out. They had golf carts to pick the arrivals up and bring them over to the helicopter. Then once they had landed at the site. There was a person there to greet them, as well as offer them something to drink. Cindy's team had spent two days with Joe going through the entire project. Really getting to know the entire complex. He had shown them all the key items of the project. Getting to know the facility inside and out. And learning about all the many amenities that will be offered to the future owners. And Cindy talked to her team about pricing. Her team was all top-notch. One of the sales agent would stay with the client from the moment that they had landed. Cindy would be there to greet everyone and be in charge of the paperwork. Joe and I sat back and nervously waited on pins and needles. I really had hoped that we sold all 51 units today. Joe and I stacked everything we had, to finance this project. I guess at this point it was out of are hands, and all up to Cindy and her team.

    We had given all the construction workers an entire paid week off. So that they wouldn't be in the way. Before we did however, Jack had them clean the place spotless, and make sure that the complex was safe for visitors. There was a tent set up, were the chef, and his staff had prepared a whole lot of good food. And a bartender to provide drinks. Cindy had been working with the chef. We weren't sparing any expense, on the food or booze. She wanted to wine and dine the prospective clients.

So, all the floors were now poured, so the project had moved to the next phase of construction process. So, this was the perfect time to be showing the clients the complex. The elevators were now installed in each tower, is what we were now calling them. The hydroponic floor heat was now working. So, the facility would be a perfect seventy-two degrees as the tour were taking place. Most of the lighting was installed.

I let Cindy's agents do their jobs, it was clear they knew what they were doing. It was tough to just have to hang back and watch this all unfolding, and not being in charge of what was now happen. I did have the occasional question coming from clients. People that we had met at the wedding had come up and said hi to me. Joe and I had tried to say hi to all the clients when they had first arrived. It was about all that Cindy would allow us to do.

A couple hours after the viewing had started, having no idea how things were going. Cindy called Joe and I over. I asked her what's up?

"Well, I just thought that you two would want to know that we have already sold ten of the condos. They all are good firm offers. All cash offers, I'm writing up the contracts now. But it gets even better boys! We sold them each for six million. A full million over what we originally had planned of asking per unit! And it gets even better guys, we raised the yearly maintenance fee up to six-hundred-and fifty thousand. A hundred and fifty thousand dollars more per unit."

"Holly shit honey! That is absolutely amazing! We are going to clean up thanks to you."

"I know, I'm sure that you'll find a way to thanks me later! How about a good foot massage? Because I sure could use one. Oh, and some pickles, and vanilla ice cream. What it's pregnancy cravings."

More potential clients were showing up now. Every single one of Cindy's agents were with clients. Joe and I were very nervous and excited all at the same time. I enjoyed sitting back and watching Cindy, and her team in their element.

Over the next couple hours, surprisingly twenty more units ended up selling. We only had thirteen units now still left. I couldn't believe just how good it was going, and we still a whole lot of interest still happening, with several more clients still here, and yet coming. So, this is Cindy in her element. She started a bidding war for the remainder of the units. The next five units went for six point five million. And then the next four ended up going for a full seven million.

   So, by four, we only had three more units now still left. And we had eight couples that were still very much interested. And it was up to who had wanted the last three the most. After very intense negations the next condo sold for seven-in-a-half-million. The second to the last price jumped up to eight million. Now with only one condo now left. More and more money was being offered up. The final unbelievable price for the last condo was an unbelievable twelve million. I just about shit myself; three times more than I had plan on what it would sell for.

   We made an additional fifty-nine-and-a-half million dollars. So, Joe and I were very excited by completely selling out! Joe and I didn't know how much more that we had actually ended up making. About an hour after everyone had left. Cindy and her team met, and went over paperwork, so Joe and I went and got a couple of drinks. I was so nervously excited, that I could barely sit still. I was on pins and needles at the moment.

Then Cindy's assistant Meagan came and got us both. The two of us came and sat down across the table from Cindy. "Well boys you want to know the final numbers. I know that you're going to be pleasantly surprised."

"Hell, yes we want to know!"

"First of all, I would like to say congratulation as the units are now officially sold out, my team and I continued to raise the condo's price. Are you boys ready to hear the news, well here it goes, We made and additional fifty-nine-in-a-half-million dollars additional in overall profit! of course before commissions, and taxes are subtracted."

I just about shit myself! Wholly crap! Way to go, I had no idea that we would have made this kind of money!" Then instantly I began wondering what to do with all these profits. But then Cindy had more news for the both of us!

"Wait I'm not done just yet, I raised the yearly maintenance fee from half a million, to three-quarters of a million. That's an extra one point two seven five million a year. Guaranteed for twenty years. I know we spoke of ten, but we increased the contract time. Not so shabby right? So, a grand total of $314,500,000, plus the condo dad bought for five million, a grand total of $319,500,000. In total sales!"

   I just about collapsed hearing such numbers. I'm estimating total build cost at around $135,000,000. After commission and taxes. We should net out around $92,000,000 profit, not too shabby. Hell, I'm already thinking about the next project already. The gears in my head now turning.

   Honey, you, and your team did an amazing job here today. I want to thank you and your team. Honey call them all in here, I would like to have a talk with them. They all ended up coming into the office. Before they did, Joe and I talked it over.

   "So, my brother and I and I think Cindy would agree, that you all did an amazing job here today. And we just wanted to personally thank you all for all your hard work, we all make some damn good money here today.

   Now I will need you to work with your clients on how they would like to do their interiors of their condos. We also want to give you each an additional $50,00 bonus, as a way to say thank you for all your hard work. And doing a great job."

pg. 96

They all liked that, Cindy glanced over and smiled at me. "But enough business for the day. Let's all go have a nice dinner, and some drinks.

CHAPTER TEN:

"Fully Complete"

It took another six months to fully complete the entire project out. So, we had decided to go ahead and hold a little celebration. We had planned on having an open house weekend, have all the owner come out and stay if they had wanted to come and spend the weekend in their very own condo's. Which are fully furnished. Picked out by the owners, Right down to the dishes, and silverware. When they come, we are encouraging them to go ahead and move in their personal items. We had planned on throwing a party. Almost all the owners had loved the idea. I wanted to make this a fun time for them. We had several events planned on over the course of the weekend, like a pool party, movie night, and a dance, and a couple of chef cooked meals. Cindy had a welcoming gift basket left in each of the owner's condos.

The first owners started arriving around noon time on Friday afternoon. I hired extra help for the weekend. Especially providing the condo owners help with carrying anything like luggage down to their new condo's. I just wanted the experience to be an enjoyable one for all of them. If they had a good time, and enjoyed their condo's, then if something tragically were to say happen, they then wouldn't be so hesitant on taking shelter in the shelter if the time sadly does end up tragically coming.

Two separate owners couldn't actually attend this weekend, due to prior commitments. So, I arrange another time to meet with them at a later date and time.

The blast doors would be remaining open for the duration of the weekend. If the owners weren't on the list, the security wouldn't be letting them pass on through the gate. At seven we were holding a formal dinner in the great room. Lots of good food. Once everyone had arrived and was seated and had their drinks. Cindy and I went up on stage, to say a few words. Cindy spoke first.

"Hello everyone! I'm so happy to see you all here tonight. Please try and enjoy all the amenities while you're here this weekend. And if you have any questions whatsoever, please feel free to ask one of us. Now I know my husband wants to say a few words to you all. I look forward to chatting with you all one on one."

"I first wanted to welcome everyone here tonight. I hope you are all happy with how your condo's, and the way the complex came out. If anyone would like to take a tour just let Joe, Dave, or I know. I'm here all weekend. So now I would like to talk about why it is we all bought a condo here in the first place. To protect ourselves if anything seriously goes wrong in the world. This place will protect us all. It is my job to protect you all while you stay with us. God forbid that day ever comes if it does.

I have an app that I want you all to download onto your phones. In the event that there is an actual emergency. This app will notify you all immediately; it will give you very specific instructions on what you should do in the event of an actual emergency. You all need to understand if this app ends up warning you. You should take this alert very seriously. If you do receive this. Please understand, there will not be much time to make it here. You have to drop whatever you're currently doing and get here. I recommend that you bring whatever items you may want with you, clothing pictures, personal care items ahead of time. Check with Dave head of security. He can help you make any necessary arrangements. If you so desire to ship the items here, and we will personally take your items to you condo's.

Make no mistake ladies and gentlemen, if you choose to protect yourself, you must leave everything you covet behind, to save yourselves. Items can be replaced, life cannot. Depending on the severity of the particular threat, will depend on just how long the blast doors will remain locked. Once we are all inside, and the blast doors in fact do close. The system will not open the doors back up again until the predesignated time has fully passed. The longest period the doors will remain closed is for is five years. This would mean that it was something very serios, like say Thermo-nuclear war. This place is set up for all our protection. Before you leave this weekend, we will assist you on downloading the app to all your phones. As well as test to make sure that it's functioning correctly.

One more thing, we will need by the end of this weekend to know anyone that will be joining you. If you do not identify them to us ahead of time, under no circumstances will they be let in at the time of the actual emergency. Everyone retina will need to be scanned into our system, in order to be allowed access. No one not in the system will be allowed in under no circumstance. So please make an appointment with Dave before you leave this weekend. Please feel free if you have any questions, please come to me, Dave, or Joe. Tomorrow at noon I would like to meet back here. I want to go over with you all, what exactly it will be like if you are being summoned here. Now, I see the foods ready, so I'll let you all eat and enjoy your food."

At noon, the next day. Everyone had arrived at my meeting. I began once everyone had arrived. "I want to thank everyone for coming. I hoped you all enjoyed your fist night in the condo. I understand that the subject matter of this meeting is quite heavy, but we all need to be prepared for the what if. After all that's why you all bought a condo in such a facility.

I really need you all to try and comprehend what exactly it's going to mean when the warning comes on your phone. If you choose to join us. Then you are choosing to be a survivor. But make no mistake ladies and gentlemen. This also will mean that you will be leaving behind everything that you own and hold dear to you. Everyone that you know, all behind. There would be a very good chance everything would be destroyed in the impending doom. The world you are leaving behind, may look a whole lot different, once we do finally emerge once more. So, if you do choose to save yourselves. Understand all that you will be giving up. And as nice as this place is. You're going to have to be inside here for a very long time. Physically, and mentally, this is going to take a real heavy toll on each and every one of us, I'm sure. No one will blame you if you think this would be too high of price to pay. I would completely understand if you had any misgivings at all. But understand if you change your mind, and don't join us. There would be a very likely chance that you wouldn't end up surviving yourself.

    I will tell you one thing. I have the money, and the ability to save myself if the time comes, and you can sure believe you me, I will choose to survive. Is that a crime, no I say it's not. We have every right to want to continue to stay alive. I choose to be a survivor. I don't choose to die, because of the stupidity, and evils of others. And wonder if it's a meteor strike. Your odds of surviving inside here are far, far greater. That's exactly why I built this facility to save myself, and other like-minded people that think the same as me. So, you need to be complete honestly with yourselves, and ask yourselves is this too what you want. Are you willing to give up everything, in order to save yourselves. You should all consider your answer very carefully. Don't take this decision lightly. So, when and if the times comes, you will know what to do. I am at peace with my own decision, you must all be with your own decision as well. Because whatever your choice is, it will become irreversible.

By the end of the weekend, it was quite clear that everyone there was all in. we wrapped up the weekend around noon on Sunday. Cindy and I didn't stick around long afterwards. Cindy's parents are at our house babysitting our daughter. So, we both wanted to get back home to her. We were both missing her. But it was nice to actually be able to get some uninterrupted sleep for a change. Something neither of us get these days. I had forgotten how much I had missed that.

CHAPTER ELEVEN:

"The Signal None Of Us Wanted To Receive"

It had been more than sixteen months since the complex had been fully now finished. For the most part, we have all gone on with our normal lives. I have been in the early stages of constructing a second adventure into a nuclear shelter, after the success of our first. This time up in Montana. The complex would be slightly larger. I had learned a lot from the first one. What to do, and not to do.

The situation around the world has been progressively have gotten much worse over the last year, quite worrisome in fact. Tensions with the world superpowers are growing ever more strained by the day. The Russians are trying to stop the ever advancement of the Ukrainian forces, as they are now advancing into Russia soil, as the war they had started has gone so drastically wrong for them. There is a real worry that Putin will become desperate enough to employee their nuclear weapons against Ukraine to hold off this unexpected invasion into their mother land.

Then at the same time, China is getting even more embolden, and is now preparing to invade Taiwan. Over the last several months they have been moving soldiers, and military assets just off the coast of Taiwan, over on the mainland. Which means the United States is preparing for a possible war with China to defend Taiwan. As the United States has been re-deploying more soldiers, and military equipment to the south Pacific. It was clear what their agenda ultimately is.

Then if that wasn't bad enough, North Korea has also become more embroiled, and from satellite images, it looks like they are preparing for war against South Korea, and the Unites States. They have been amassing their soldiers all along the De-militarized zone.

Then things in our own country wasn't looking so good either. The country was further divided since the possibly Civil war looms even closer. It seems like the leadership is proving to be quite useless, and ineffective in their leadership. Which is weakening the strength of the United States in the eyes of the rest of the world, as the country is possibly preparing to fight a war on several different fronts all at once, including our own. It's clear that our enemies wants to take advantage of Americans current weakness in its leadership; they want to overwhelm American forces on several different fronts all at once. Knowing that American forces couldn't possibly fend off so much, not all at once. Surely planning on actually attacking us on American soil. Our enemies goal.

I was growing quite worried, that World War Three was now on the verge of starting at any time now.

It was a Saturday morning; November 15th, 2023. I was relaxing and drinking coffee and watching CNN. When the worst possible thing could possibly have happened. And then an emergency broadcast over the phone, and Television, and radio. And on the TV. The emergency broadcast network. The warning was coming from the North Koreans who had just launched a massive military attack on South Korea. And Long-range mobile launch pads carrying thermo-nuclear missiles in North Korea were being prepared to being launched. They are North Koreans next generation missiles. Which now are quite capable of striking anywhere on the

West Coast of the United States. I had a reliable source at the Pentagon, they informed me that both American, and South Korean forces are preparing to move on the North Koreans. Before they can fire off the first missiles. In coordination with the North Koreans, the Chinese according to defense satellites, were starting to move their forces. At the same time there has been detection of Russian mobile missile launchers, of their intercontinental thermos-nuclear missions were being redeployed. That could only mean that Putin was preparing to use them. In turn NATO was starting to prepare its own forces for war against Russia, China, North Korea. It was clear, within just hours, under utter madness, World War Three was surely now breaking out right in front of our eyes. And I fear there may be nothing left by the end of this day.

    Left with no other choice. I had Dave send out the signal to the others, and then have him begin to prepare for everyone impending immediate arrivals. Maybe I should have waited longer first, but if I did. I might become too late.

    Luckily both Cindy and I were at home at the time. I contacted Joe, his Family, and mine in utter disbelief, and in shock. As we quickly packed, and then rushed to the airport, breaking the speed limit all the way there. Our pilot was already for us. It was clear people were freaking out. That they were about to be wiped off the face of the map. We were in the air thirty minutes after the emergency warning was sent out. Two hours later we landed and then immediately took our helicopter out to the complex. Once we had landed, Dave was there to greet us. We were all in a somber mood, as the reality of the situation was certainly setting in. I grabbed my daughter, and we all then rushed and ran inside. All our hands were full of stuff. I carried our daughter; our dog Kona came along with us. We couldn't leave him behind.

Others were also arriving, and more were flooding in rather quickly. Others had arrived before us. Joe and I both came out to assist Dave with everyone that was arriving. Meanwhile Cindy took our daughter down to our condo.

"Dave how many more are still due in?"

We still have eleven more owners that are still outstanding! I hope they hurry on up." He looked down at his watch, "The blast doors are automatically shutting in thirty-two minutes time, and I can't stop the count down at this point.

pg. 109

Once the process was started, it becomes automated at this point."

"I hope they can make it in time. Dave what's the latest on the Chinese or North Koreans?"

"Well Ten minutes ago, satellites detected ten separate missiles launched in North Korea. They are coming towards the United States west coast. China began an invasion in Taiwan. At the same time Russia has just fired off several of their own ICM missiles. In response the United States had countered, by sending off our own nuclear warheads directed towards both Russia, and North Korea! And China. They call it mutual destruction. In this scenario neither side survives."

Dave how long do we have until the first missile ends up striking the United states, and do we know where these missiles will strike?"

Dave looked down at his watch. Thirty-five minutes. So far, we know that LA, San Francisco, Las Vegas, Portland, and two in the Seattle area. They are going after Banger naval base, and fort Lewis-McCord military bases, to try and wipe out our nuclear submarines currently in port. But luckily all the subs were deployed two days ago. The subs will be firing all their warheads once in range. San Diego naval base. They are also going after Pearl Harbor, both of these also both seem to be a target!"

"My God! Mankind has really gone and now done it haven't they. We are going to annihilate one another. I just can't believe this. I fear the end of the world is gravely now upon us. What the hell have we all done? Within hours it all could be gone, and for what. There won't be any winners!"

I just stood outside as long as I could taking in the fresh air, and the beauty of the outside world. I knew there was a very good chance I would never see it like this ever again. After the missiles started striking.

I just sincerely hoped the other owners can make it here in time. Almost everyone had arrived. But three owners were still outstanding. The time was running out for them. According to the apps on their phones, which we have the ability to track. They were growing really close. There was just two more minutes before the doors automatically would be closing. Two of the three owners made it safely inside, and their families had arrived just as the nick of time. I screamed for them to hurry up. The last owns pulled up in front of the doors. They couldn't get a close parking spot. But the doors were now already starting to now slowly close. They ran as fast as they possibly could to try and make it inside in time. The female just barely had squeezed through the small opening in the nick of time. The husband had been twenty feet behind her. It was unfortunately too late for him. He tried, but the doors closed shut, and locked tightly, without him making it through, if he would have tried. He would have been surely crushed to death.

She screamed out when she had realized he hadn't made it in time! She had thought that he was directly behind her, but when he was running towards the door, he had tripped, he got back up, but not quick enough. If he wouldn't have tripped he would have been ok.

"Robert, You have to open the god damn doors, and let him in. Please you have to. He's going to die out there! Don't you get it. I don't want to survive without him. You hear me, now open the fucking doors! Name your price, I'll give you anything, if you'll save him!"

Dave and I tried to calm her! "I'm so sorry, but we aren't able to override the blast doors at this time. Ms. Johnston, You see that timer on the wall. It means that the doors will not open up again for five years from now, before they will open back up again. I'm truly very sorry for your loss. But this is just the way that it is.

She balled hard, other women came over and did their best to try and calm and comfort her. In the end, she had become so inconsolable that we gave her a sedative, and brought her to her condo, so she could rest.

Over the loudspeakers, "Ladies and Gentlemen please let's all try and remain calm, we are now all in this together. We must try and be there for one another. To get through this most tragic times, we are all a family now, whether we like it or not. I would like if we all could meet up in the great hall at this time."

I took the stage. "Please everyone please come site down. I honestly hoped that this day would never have arrived. But sadly, it has. I know that we are all quite scared and upset by these unfolding events. But I ensure you all. That we will all be quite safe in here. No matter what happens out there. I say we should all pray." Everyone bowed their heads, and remained silent, as we all said a silent prayer.

Once everyone was done praying, "Now because of the severity of the threat taking on out there. The blast door will not open back up again for the next five years. I know that that sounds like a very long time at the moment." Everyone gasped when they heard how long we would have to remain locked up in here. "But we will at least all have a good life while we are staying here. We will make you as comfortable as we possibly can during this time. We need to try and remember that we are all survivors. We will need to remain strong, so once we are finally outside, we will have a chance to start over once more. It may be up to us, to repopulate the world once more, I certainly don't hope that it has come to this. Hopefully there will be other survivors, but we will have no way of possibly knowing that until the doors open up again. We suspect that after all the nuclear missiles go off. A nuclear winter will be created, which will devastate the climate all around the world, for many years to come. If so though we would no longer be locked inside. We would have the protection of the complex, and still be able to feed ourselves in such an event was to occur.

Now everyone, the book of the rules that you were all provided will be enforced to try and maintain peace and order while we are all in here. We will all be assigned jobs to help keep all this going smoothly. Please all take the time to study the rules. I suggest that we all go to our own condos, unpack. And be with our loved ones. Get yourself situated, and comfortable, and we can all meet back up in a couple of days. It's going to take time for us all to except what's just happened to us, and get use to this new life of ours. This is difficult on all of us. There is food stocked in your condos. So please. Go be with your families now. We should all be quite thankful, that we will survive this. We need to try and remember this fact."

   As the people began exiting the great room. Everyone had a rather somber, defeated look present on their faces. No one was talking much. Dave then came and pulled Joe and I aside. I just thought you should know that by now. All the nuclear war heads should have stricken all their intended targets around the world. In all likelihood millions upon millions of people are probably now dead, and millions more will end up dying from the nuclear fallout, in the coming days.

Countless cities have been wiped off the face of the map. More than likely, with that many warheads going off all at once. The survives will be facing a nuclear winter. The United States would have sent the rest of their warheads off before it was too late. The last to fire off there warheads will be all are nuclear subs. What they call mutual annihilation. Russia and China would have done the very same thing. So, in the end, there are no winners, only losers. In shock, I can't believe that we had finally gone and done it. So, senseless.

Unfortunately, we have no real way of actually knowing for sure once the blast doors had shut. All ties to the outside world were completely now severed, including all the outside security cameras on the outside of the complex. I wish we wouldn't have designed it in this way. It would have been helpful if we could see the going on outside, and possibly still communicate with the outside world, if it was even still possible.

Suddenly five years seemed like a very, very long time. I looked around and thought that this is a mistake perhaps. I mean what if just by chance it didn't get as bad as we had thought. We don't actually have any, actual proof. Anyway, of proving it. Then all this will all be a huge mistake.

And if it really got that bad, I wondered if it was a huge mistake to try and survive. So, what will we do in five years, when the doors finally do open up again. There may be nothing still around to return too!! The radiation levels may be much too high, that it wouldn't be safe for us to ever be able to leave the shelter. We may never be able to leave this place. We did purchase radiation suites, and Geiger counters. So, we will have the ability to check when the day does come to attempt to leave. We will need to know if it's safe or not.

CHAPTER TWELVE:
"Getting Use To This New Life"

I didn't sleep at all on our first night on the inside. With the thought of what's happened on the outside world, it was horrifying to me, that it had actually come to all this. And then I couldn't stop thinking about that stupid god damn count down cloak of all things. Maybe that was a bad idea. It was going to make this all feel like a prison sentence I'm afraid as time goes on. We would have to be in here 1825 days. That is an awful lot of days to be locked up. And it would be a constant reminder.

It was still quite early in the morning; Cindy and my daughter were still asleep. And since I hadn't fallen asleep, I decided to just get up, and go ahead and take a walk around, check in on everything. I had to make sure everything was working properly. Maybe it was just away to calm myself. I think I was realizing that this was going to be much harder than I had imagined.

I wasn't running into anybody on my little stroll. It was eerily quiet, too quite. I realized on my stroll, that I never really had truly thought about what this would actually be like if we actually ever did end up getting locked up in here. I was being washed over with a sense of pure guilt, and utter dread. I questioned myself, was it actually fair that all of us in here get to survive, go about living our lives, when a whole lot of very good innocent people who didn't have the opportunity like us to be here, had to end up perishing, all thanks to the decisions made by others. I think that I shall truly be haunted by this. I can't just pretend that it was remotely even fair. The other thing that was bothering me, was my friends, and family that hadn't had the luxury of being able to come here. There was a real good chance that they could all be died now. I suddenly felt so guilty, I had to run to the nearest bathroom, and throw up.

   I had, had this grand idea, that once we were here. That somehow it would be like being on an extended vacation, that would just go on for a while. I didn't expect that I would be feeling horrible like this. I felt extremely guilty, and ashamed.

   I ended up going to the command center and checking to make sure that all the systems was working correctly. Of course, there was no issues of any kind.

I headed back to the condo a couple hours later. I was surprised to still not to running into a soul. Maybe everyone was feeling somber, much like me. Maybe we were all feeling guilty for being so selfish for saving ourselves. Maybe there would be a price paid for that. That statement couldn't be truer. We would all find that out later.

It was a couple of days before people started finally venturing out of their condo's, and slowly checking things out. I think at some point, people started realizing that at some point in time that they had to start living their lives once again. Regardless of how they felt about their decision. What other choice was there at this point. It was going to be five long years staying in here otherwise. We couldn't just stay in the condo's forever. Since I was in charge, I knew that I needed to pick myself up, first and foremost. I had to try and project strength and confidence, and try build everyone else's spirits up around me.

Cindy and I sat down and talked about it. She was a good person to go to for advice. In our conversation I realized just how much she too was hurting as well. "Robert what kind of a world will we be bringing are daughter into once the blast doors open up again. I'm really scared that there won't be anything left to return too. What the hell will we do then? We can't stay in this place forever!"

"Honey, I really don't know what will actually be waiting for us out there. We will just have to wait and find out, then won't we. Meanwhile we need to remember to try and live our lives. Let's try and not worry about what we currently don't have any control of. We will deal with that when the time does come. Meanwhile, we can have a pretty good life in here, if we make it good. We have all we need here to do so. We need to be there for our daughter. We have to try and give her a good life while we are in here. Because of the age we brought her here, she won't even remember the outside world. It's hard to think, that this is the only life she will know, to her, this will be normal as weird as that sounds to you and me."

"Your right Robert! I'll tell you what I'll go make some breakfast. Then maybe we could go take Meagan to the playroom later this afternoon."

After breakfast, I got together with Joe and Dave, so we could discuss the general operation.

We headed to the command center. Only Joe, Dave, Cindy, and I had the security clearance to be in this section of the complex. Food production area was only granted to those that worked in those areas. And as far as the equipment, and the storage areas were completely off limits to all.

We decided to try and get people to come out of their condos. And start being social once more. This was absolutely vital! We needed to thrive, not just survive. So, we decided to try and host some fun events to get the people to try and forget about the outside world. We decided to host a community pool party. We could barbeque hot dogs, have drinks, play music, and games. So, we had decided to invite everyone tomorrow at noon. Let people get to know one another and have something to look forward to.

We tried to simulate night and day down here. At nighttime lights would dim way down. The electronic windows would also simulate night and day, and also the different seasons. Thousands of videos were contained in the windows. We wanted to make the experience as real as possible. Make it a little easier to except being locked up in this place.

Cindy loved the idea of the pool party, she recruited her mother, and Joe's wife to help to plan, and set it up. As it turns out, they went all out. They made decorations up in the craft room.

Meanwhile Cindy's dad came over to our condo, along with joe. We put on a Disney movie on for the kids. In the living room. While the three of us went and sat in the dining room and started having a couple of drinks. We decided to play some poker, to pass the time. Cindy's dad was a real card shark as it turns out. I'm glad we were just using poker chips, and not actually playing for cash. Cash had no value down here. Probably a hard concept for all our rich condo owners to understand the concept.

The girls had been gone several hours. We decided to surprise them and go ahead and make dinner for the girls. They didn't get back until around six. After dinner we put the kids down. And then decided to go watch a movie at the theater. So, since the complex was a smart facility. We could monitor the children while they had slept. We were doing a little sleep over. We all headed over to the movie theater. We made some popcorn and poured some soda. It was nice, a couple of other of the residents decided to join us. Exactly what I had wanted to happen.

    The pool party was a real hit. The residents started to forget about the outside world. Come back out of their shells. As time went on, a routine started happening. New friendships started forming, and blossoming. People began to sign up for jobs. Or host different events. This was good to give them all something to do.

CHAPTER THIRTEEN:

"The Reality Was Starting Too Set In"

SIX MONTHS HAD PASSED:

    Cindy and a couple of the other ladies here, have set up a makeshift school for the kids we have with us. We have a total of fourteen kids ranging from two years old, up to fifteen. And surprise, surprise four of our residents are now pregnant. One of those pregnant woman, is in fact Cindy. Understand that there is a whole lot of down time here. Cindy thought it important that the kids still receive an education while they are in here. All the kids would need to learn at least the basics. reading, writing and arithmetic's, history, and maybe with a few fun subjects thrown in. Cindy was enjoying herself very much. The kids seem to enjoy it as well. Because it gives them something to do during the daytime hours. And something that we discovered was rather important, that was, having something to look forward too. Boredom was one of our worst enemies inside here. We were all affected by this from time to time.

Truth told; this place is beginning to feel a bit confining to me, more so each and every day, if I'm being honest. I have been keeping these feelings all to myself and bottled up. But to be honest. It was getting to me. I wanted to go outside in the worst way.

It was around 11pm, I was about to go to bed, when I got an unexpected frantic call from a very upset Margaret Larson one of the residences in tower two. She said it was an emergency, that I needed to come there at once. She sounded pretty hysterical. I told her I would be right there. I rushed over as quickly as I could. I knocked on the front door. Margaret was balling as she came to answer the door.

"What's going on Margaret? What seems to be wrong"?

"Oh my God, It's Bill, he's dead. He said he was having a heart attack."

"He's on the floor in the master bedroom!"

I went to him, I checked for a pulse. Before I could do anything for him, He was already gone. I ran to the hall and grabbed a defalcator machine. I tried shocking his heart, with no luck. He must have had a massive heart attack.

"My god my husband is dead! I don't want to be left alone in this hell hole, without him with me. He's the one that wanted to be here, not me, I hate this fucking place. What am I supposed to do now."

"I'm so sorry Margaret for your tragic loss."

I then called Joe, and Dave to come meet me here. I would need both their help with this.

Once they were here, we decided what we should do. We don't have a coffin to put his body in. And we couldn't bury him, even if we had one. We would have to dispose of his body. Dave went and grabbed a cart. We decided that we would wheel his body down to the incinerator. While everyone was home. So, they wouldn't have to see us moving his body. Then in a couple of days we would have a funeral for Bill. Allow everyone to say their goodbyes. We explained to Margaret what we were going to do. Joe called his wife, to come stay with her. Margaret couldn't be left alone in her current state. While we did what we needed to. I was afraid of this happening. I knew that there would be a pretty good chance of this happening at some point. I didn't want the others to see what we now going to be doing.

We had made it down to the incinerator with his body. We had to fire it up. After we placed his body inside. It took a half an hour to burn his body completely up. We decided to let it cool back down, and in the morning, we would find a small container to place his ashes in. And then we could present it to his wife at his funeral.

What the three of us would later learn over the next four in a half years, is we would end up having to do this several more times to come, sadly enough. This was only the tip of the iceberg of things to come. We would discover that this place would take a real heavy toll on all of us over enough time. There wouldn't be a single resident, that wasn't negatively affected by this place. We would discover that there was a high price for all of us to pay to simply be a survivor. Nothing in life is free as they say, a lesson that we would learn the hard way.

CHAPTER FOURTEEN:
"Life As We Know It"

NINE MONTHS IN:

Things are becoming quite plainly doll, and extremely ordinary, so bland, and beyond boring. The food we eat, doesn't even excite me any longer, and I'm normally a big foody person. We have been doing our very best to change things up the best way that we can, with what we have to work with. But really there is only so much we can do, to add some variety to what we eat. Adding different spices can only help so much.

Even though we have hundreds of thousands movies, and TV shows at our disposal. I can't ever seem to ever find anything interesting to ever watch. I'll sometimes spend an hour scrolling through the different selection, that I had already looked at hundreds of times, just trying to find something interesting to be able to watch. I really miss not being able to watch any sports. At least ones I don't already know the outcome too. It would be football season now, my favorite time of the year for sports. Both college, and pro. But I think what I am missing must is just being able to go outside, smell the fresh air, and have the sun light hitting my naked exposed a skin. Go on a hike. Or walk down along the beach. Or going crabbing. I'm an outdoor person. And being in here is darn near like being in nothing more than a nice prison.

    Sometimes it's proved to be too much on some of us being forced to be in here. I'm not sure any of us are happy any longer with our decision to hide out in here. We have sadly had two resent suicides. Two months ago. Just a few days apart from one another. First person was Ms. Watson, the woman that made it inside without her husband. Mentally she truly had never recovered from the loss of her husband. She was riddled with guilt, and extreme loneliness. So, I don't think hers was much of a surprise to any of us, I knew eventually she probably would have ended it. I always felt guilty that we weren't able to get her husband inside in time. If we had, I'm pretty sure that she would have been a completely different person, I'm sure. So, her death was squarely on me. Something I was going to have to live with for the rest of my life. She never attended any of our events. She wasn't social with anyone. She went out of her way to avoid making contact, with everyone. Then one day Dave was doing a wellness check on her. She left her front door unlocked. He sadly had ended up discovering that She had slit her wrist as she sat in her bathtub full of water. She was completely naked. It was a day before we had ended up discovering her body. It was a sickening site to have to come upon. Dave drained the water in the tub. Dave and Joe and I really hated this particular duty. And just three days after her husband's funeral. Margret had ended up hanging herself. She had used a bed sheet. She had tied one end of the sheet to the bedframe, and then over the top of her bedroom door. And first standing on a chair she then had tied it tightly around her own neck. Then she stepped off the chair, and kicked the chair over, so she couldn't chicken out. I hoped that she didn't suffer for too long, that she died quickly. Because her neck hadn't snapped, she probably had to hang there several long minutes, before finally succumbing to strangulation.

   It becoming abundantly quite clear that this place is slowly changing all of us, robbing of us of our sanity, and just maybe our souls. And certainly not changing us for the better. It's understandable why, I think it's making us all much more sinical, and hardening us. I feel as though I'm slowly being poisoned, from the inside out. One of the worst things there really isn't much work to do, the facility is pretty automated. Before coming here to live. A lot of my self-worth has always come from my career, and not the money that I made. I got a lot of pride from that. But here there is not much to do, to stay busy, other than monitoring all the equipment, feed the livestock, and distribute the food. Enough work to keep one person busy each and every day, but we divided this up amongst several people, just to insure there was something to do.

Generally, from what I have observed people in here are much more on edge. We have had a few fights break out lately. Especially between spouses. Not serious enough yet that we had to lock anyone up in a jail cell, but I fear it won't be much longer before we actually do so. We have also seen alcohol consumption on the rise. That would include me. I need something to take the edge off. Maybe stay a bit numb.

Cindy's now a very eight months pregnant. I don't advise being locked up in a bomb shelter, with an eight-month pregnant woman. That is if you possibly want to retain your sanity. She is driving me absolutely nuts.

Now when it comes to my daughter, it breaks my heart, because my three-year-old daughter doesn't have any memories of the outside world. She was to young when we brought her here. This place, as odd as it sounds, is all that she knows of the world. She has a whole lot of energy. She is non-stop on the move. But she is definitely a daddy's girl, sure enough. She is definitely a little version of me alright. She loves tagging along whenever I go anywhere. Truthfully, I love it. One of the bright spots in my life, that is for sure. Without her, this place would be completely unbearable I'm afraid.

I wish we had a doctor with us living in here. Especially to deliver the upcoming babies that are going to be on their way soon enough. I don't have a clue of what to do when the time does come. I have never actually delivered a baby.

There has been other problems that have been cropping up as of late. We have had couples that were breaking up. Surprise, surprise. As it turns out, when your around a spouse twenty-four hours a day. Seven days a week, every minute of every day. It can take a real heavy toll on a couple.

No matter how much that they are in love. Suddenly everything they do, can suddenly become quite irritating by their spouses. We started using the newly vacated condos as a place for one of the separated spouses could stay. I also wouldn't be surprised if there has been some cheating currently taking place amongst some of the couples here. Unfortunately, the evils of man, managed to have followed us inside. And with each new day, it was ridding its ugly head, more and more all the time.

    One thing I do every single day, is I go and look at the damn cloak we have been in here now for **277 days**, and the doors won't open back up again for another **1,548 days**. Which to me now seems like an eternity to me at this point in time. I was seriously struggling with this. This place feels more like a fucking prison, than anything else.

    To try and coupe with this place, I tried to at least find one positive thing each and every day. That wasn't always an easy task some days. This did help me a little. Because I was the leader of this place. It was tough on me. Because I had to always be extra strong and remain positive and try to motivate the others to come out of their shells. They all expect me to be strong for them. And because I was the leader, people did turn to me when they needed to find someone to talk to, or simply just vent to someone. They felt quite comfortable enough coming to me with their personal problems. If it made them feel better coming to me, then so be it.

One of my routines was to go workout, after I woke up every single morning. One to keep in shape, then the other it was a way to take out my frustrations out with physical exercise.

I could tell that this place was taken a real toll on Joe. he seems to get easily agitated these days. Which normally wasn't like him. He was normally a very easy-going person. So, I began keeping an eye on him. I really hoped that we would be able to make it all the way.

I just know by what I have been seeing taking place in this place wouldn't eventually become a powder keg. And when that day does arrive, we should become very scared.

CHAPTER FIFTTEEN:

"Tragic Loss"

Our baby was now officially coming, whether or not we were ready for it. The girls came over, to try and assist Cindy with the childbirth. I of course was a nervous wreck. We had to rely on one another, without the benefit of a doctor as a resident. Cindy's water had broken. And her labor pains had started. This all started about four am. By noon not much progress had been made. I was a complete nervous wreck by this point. Catherine had taken charge of things. Having birth four children herself. She certainly knew more than me.

Catherine thought that Cindy may be fully dilated finally. But when she was reaching inside, she unexpectedly had realized that the baby was currently breached. She suddenly was a bit worried. If she couldn't get the baby turned around, then we would be in real trouble. She had to somehow try and get the baby turned back around. Normally if this were to happen. The doctor would do a see section. But we didn't have the luxury of doing that. Catherine had medical gloves on, and she lubed the gloves up.

"Ok now honey this is going to hurt a bit, but we have to try and get the baby turned around. I don't want you trying to push, while I'm doing this. Are you ready?"

"Yes, go ahead!"

Catherine then slowly reached her right hand inside. Oh, I can feel the babies' feet!"

Cindy screamed out in pain! I knew it was hurting her, but this was the only way. I held on to her hand and did my best to try comfort her through all the pain. I knew that I wasn't being much help.

"Ok honey try and relax for me. Now that I have ahold of the baby, I'm now going to try and turn your baby around now. I can feel the baby now moving."

It took her a couple of minutes to get the baby turned back around the right way. I can now fell the baby's head the right way. Cindy had looked quite pale at this point. She was clearly completely exhausted. And she was doing this natural. This wasn't by choice.

pg. 137

"Cindy are you ready to start and try pushing again?"

"Yes, I want to get this baby out of me now. I'm so tired. I don't remember feeling like this when my daughter was born."

"Ok, honey, go ahead and start pushing now, I'll tell you when to stop."

After a couple of difficult pushes, "Cindy good news! The baby's head is starting to crown now. Very good, now go ahead and start pushing again for me, your doing so good. Very good the baby's head is now partly now out. Oh my gosh, Your baby has a full head of hair. Ok now push again for me! Very good sweetie!"

Cindy screamed out. The worse part was that Cindy had to do this childbirth naturally. We weren't able to give her an epidural. So, she was in a whole lot of pain.

"Ok, Cindy push hard for me, once the shoulders are clear, it will go real fast after that."

Cindy pushed really hard, That's when Catherine noticed that the umbilical cord was completely wrapped tightly around the baby's neck, she knew that they had to hurry, this was quite serios at this point, but she didn't want to worry, or alarm Cindy at this point, she needed her to try and stay focus. The baby was turning blue, which means it been cut off of oxygen for a while from the look of the baby's complexion.

As Cindy pushed through hard again. Catherine now desperate to help save the baby pulled on the baby at the same time. Soon as Cindy's baby boy was free from his mother. Catharine grabbed the lifeless baby, quietly cut the umbellule cord, and unwrapped it from around the baby's neck, and then tried to quickly administer CPR on the baby.

"Catherine, what's wrong with my baby? What are you doing to my baby?"

I responded to her, I went over and held her hand. "Honey, he's not breathing! Catherine is doing First aid on him! Don't worry honey!"

Cindy looked extremely exhausted herself! She was quite pale. I had to watch on as Catherine tried her best to save my son. I held onto Cindy's hand. She was so weak, that she couldn't hold her arm up any longer. It was then that I realized that there was something definitely wrong with her. Then I looked down and noticed that there was a whole lot of blood. I knew that there shouldn't possibly be that much.

Cindy crying, said, "Please save are son, please!"

All through after more than ten solid desperate minutes, there was no sign of life. He had gone to long without oxygen I'm afraid. "Robert, I am so sorry, but he is gone. I tried, I'm so, so sorry!" Catherine was balling nearly uncontrollable at this point. She had tried everything she knew to save her nephew.

Just about the same time, Cindy suddenly, and very unexpectedly health took a turn for the worse as soon as she had heard that her baby son hadn't make it. She suddenly closed her own eyes, her hand grew suddenly cold to the touch, and the life in her, completely had slipped away without any warning whatsoever. We tried everything we could do to save her, but sadly to say, she too was now gone as well, just like that. I couldn't believe it. There had been so much blood loss.

I think that I would have cried, but I was a bit of being in complete shock at the moment. So, I guess I just couldn't believe, or for that matter except what had just happened. what had all gone down. It wasn't fair! I just left are bedroom, walked thru the living room were Cindy's parents were now crying upon hearing the tragic news. I strolled right by them, as if they weren't even there in the room. I didn't even glance over at them as I walked by them. I didn't say a single word. I had no real idea where I was even going at the moment, but I was going away from there! This was all my fault. I kept telling myself this.

   Joe was babysitting my daughter while all this had happened. I just wanted to be left alone. I didn't want to be around anyone at the moment. How is one supposed to deal with losing the two loves of your life, not to mention, losing a child. No one should have to go through that. It wasn't fair I tell you, not by a long shot. I have now lost two wives now. I went down to the bar, and then began drinking hard. I wanted to be left alone. At one point Joe came looking for me. Oh, he had found me. I argued with him, and then yelled at him to go to hell, and leave me the fuck alone. I wasn't in the right frame of mind to be around anyone at the moment. I certainly hadn't meant what I had said to him. He knew I wasn't in the right frame of mind, so he understood I was just hurting. I drank for several more hours, before I then finally ended up passing out from consuming to much alcohol. At some point while I was blacked out on the bars floor. I was brought back to my own bed at some point. I was severally hung over the whole next day. I just wasn't in a state of mind that I could be around my daughter. I know I should be, but I just didn't have it in me. I didn't want to talk to anyone. I had completely shut down.

   There was only one thing I asked for after waking up the next day, I asked Dave, and Joe to take care of Cindy's and my babies boy's body for me. That would be too much on me to bear witness too. I didn't want to be there when they did. As it turns out. They had removed both their bodies yesterday. Her parents didn't want to be present when their bodies were cremated either. I knew this was devastating to them as well, but I just wanted to be left alone. My daughter stayed at my brothers. At least she had her cousins to play with. And her aunt and uncle. They could keep her distracted at least for the time being.

   I didn't leave the condo for a good solid week, I didn't take any visitors, or even want to talk to anyone for that matter. I was being quite selfish. I knew; I couldn't help myself. I knew that this must be really hard on my daughter. I wasn't really sleeping, in plain truth, I was a total wreck, spiraling downwards.

CHAPTER SIXTEEN:
"Change In Character"

    Several painful difficult, very lonely, grueling months had passed by since the death of Cindy. Upon her death, and the fact of having to be locked up in this god damn forsaken hell hole. I was no longer the same person that first came here. Truthfully at this point in time. I would have brother taken my chances on the outside. That is if I could have done it all over again. We know that's not happening.

    Eventually as time went on after Cindy's death. I started putting all my energy into spending more time running this place. Less time on being close to anyone, including my brother Joe. In fact, my daughter has been staying with her grandparents, and Joe, and his family, I just don't have it in me to try and be a father to her at present time. As cold as it sounds, when I see her, it's like looking at a young version of Cindy. Ever her personality is much the same. A part of me died the night my wife and son had died. I haven't allowed myself to grieve or heal. I get drunk nearly every night. The good, loving side of me, seems to be now gone. What was left behind, is a bitter, negative very unhappy person who really doesn't want to be alive, or here for that matter. A person that I know for certain that Cindy wouldn't have loved. I'm not sure if it's even possible for the fun loving me to ever come back. Hell, I'm not even sure I can make it mentally the remainder of the time we still have left to be locked up inside here.

I was much more callous, uncaring towards everyone around me. I started to really enforce the rules. Beyond what I should, but I had no patients left. I took it upon myself to keep everyone in line. I wanted everyone to know their place here. And there was no longer going to be a free rides. I had concluded that we must all pull are weight. And he who controls the food, controls the masses.

This place was really starting to take a real heavy toll on some of us, much more than others. The community has experienced three more additional suicides as a result of having to be locked away in here. And two more couples have now split up. Both couples had broken up when one husband, cheated on his wife, with a wife of another couple. I was called in, when one of the husbands confronted the other husband, who had been cheating with his wife. It took Dave, and I to break them both up. They had gotten in a rather heated fist fight. We broke up the fight up and had ended up arresting the guy that had started cheating with the other guy's wife. We could understand why the other guy had started the fight. Frankly I didn't blame him at all, I would have done the very same thing. I really didn't take to kindly to it in fact. Truth told I thought that he was a real piece of shit dirt bag. Hell, I wanted to smack him around.

    We wanted to set an example. We took him and locked his ass up. I sentenced him to be locked up for three days. Though I wasn't done with him just yet. He really got under my skin. The cheating wife wasn't going to go unpunished either. I sentenced her to clean all the residences toilets for the next month. I wanted everyone to now know that this sort of behavior wasn't going to be permitted any longer. I also was going to cut them both off from the better food. Neither one of them had liked it. But I was going to go one step further than just that. The cheating spouses would not be permitted back into either of their condos. They would be permitted to get their personal items and then would have to live in a vacant condo by themselves. They would not be permitted to hook up again. If they were caught hooking up, then a harsher punishment would be handed down by the entire community. Being so isolated it was easier to convince the others to go along with me.

I didn't know it at the time, but I was slowly starting to create a dictatorship inside here. And It was becoming like a drug to me. I was addicted to unadulterated power.

CHAPERTER SEVENTEEN:

"Murder"

THIRTY MONTHS IN:

So today marked a very special day for all of us in here, we have now somehow been in this hell hole now which is **912.5** days, and we have **912.5** to go. Which in simple turns, means that we officially, it was all downhill from here. Of course, you could also look at it like we still had **912.5** days to still go. I looked at it like the cup being half full.

Being in here is taking a real toll on all of us. Much like when people have gone to prison, it has changed us all, it harden us. Sadly, many couples have broken up as a result of this fucking hell hole. Social norms are in fact breaking down inside here. We are changing as well, not for the better. Fights are regularly breaking out now. To be honest, everything is breaking down. I miss Cindy so much. I barely have been spending time with my daughter because it's much too painful, because every day she looks even more like her mom. I'm not sure if I have the capacity to love anymore any longer. I do feel guilty for not raising her myself. But I guess I brother get drunk each night. I try to stay numb.

   Yesterday when a guy here couldn't take his wives nagging any longer. They had been watching a movie in the theater, when Ms. Larson was talking through the movie, while her husband was trying to watch a movie. He had asked her to shut up several separate different times, and I guess he just finally had enough of her running her mouth, when she wouldn't shut up, he completely had ended up snapping. He ended up beating her to death with his bare hands. Her lifeless body laid their on the floor, where he had left her right between the row of chairs. He came out of the theater, with blood all over his hands. He came from out of the theater laughing loudly, "I finally got that fucking bitch to shut the fuck up, she won't talk during a movie ever again. Not after what I had done to her. It was the only way to shut her up. Then he just went and sat down on a bench outside the theater. Just laughing aloud to himself. Happy by what he had just done. Other residents that had been in the theater had first-handedly witnessing this, had then alerted me to what had just happened. I went and grabbed a gun, and handcuffs, just in case he puts up a fight. I called Joe and Dave to come give me a hand.

It was a real shame, before coming here. Him and his wife had been happily married thirty plus years. And were very much in love. But after coming in here. This place began wearing on them both. About a year ago, the arguments had started, and ever since its only escalated from there. They grew to literally hate and detest one another.

Upon hearing this, several of us had now gathered, and captured him. We were immediately going to hold an immediate trial. This was to be our first murder in here, so we were in uncharted waters here. I had all the adults gather in the great hall.

"Thank you for all coming here today. I wish we were meeting under better circumstances, other than this. So, you have all heard what has happened here tonight. I have called you all here to decide the fate of Mr. Larson, who has freely admitted that he has just brutally murdered his wife, with his bare hands. So, we are now gathered here to decide on whether he killed his wife. But we are going to decide his fate for murder. So, on the piece of paper that I will be handing out, you will write down what you want his punishment to be. We will decide as a group what his fate shall therefore be.

Let also decide options for punishment. So, raise your hand with ideas, and we will choose the 3 most popular ideas, and then we can then vote on his fate. So let me hear your idea's. Raise your hand if you have an idea.

Ralph, I see you have your hand raised, what's your idea?"

"Locking him up the remainder of the days in here, lock him up in a jail cell, and only provide his basic rations."

"very good."

"Anyone else?"

"Susan, what's your idea?"

"Execution, by hanging!"

"Ok, and anyone else?"

"torture him!"

"Ok anyone else?"

No one else raised their hands, "Ok then now that we have our three options as punishments.

Don't take your decision lightly, let's go ahead and cast are vote. Once this is decided. His punishment will be passed down today after we are done voting. There is no reason to wait casting sentence any longer. I am now going to hand out a piece of paper, write your selection down, then I will come around and gather the paper from you. Once you have written down your choice. Then fold your paper in half. Then I will count the votes."

"Ok ladies and gentlemen let's begin, shall we. The first vote, hanging. The second vote is hanging, the third vote is hanging."

With a total of fifty eights votes cast. Forty-seven said hanging, seven were for torture, and then three were for locking him up. "Well ladies and gentlemen we have are decision. Mr. Larsons fate is now decided. Let's get set up for the hanging. So, We rigged a rope up right there in the great room ceiling and we brought over an eight-foot-tall step latter. I asked everyone to remain and observe the hanging. I wanted all the adults to witness this. I wanted to send a powerful message here today firsthand. Joe and Dave went and retrieved Mr. Larson. As they brought his back he was in handcuffs.

Everyone had formed a large circle around the rope, and Mr. Larson was now standing inside it. I then spoke up, so everyone could hear me, "Mr. Larson you are guilty of murdering your wife in cold blood, as such we have decided as a group that you shall therefore immediately be put to death by hanging, for your brutal crime!"

"No, please I didn't mean it, no please don't do this."

"Mr. Larson at this time you are formally sentenced to death by hanging. Gentlemen, prepare the criminal to receive his sentence."

They brought him over to the rope tied it tightly around his neck. "Mr. Larson climb up the ladder please."

"No, please don't do this! Have you all gone completely mad?"

Everyone showing no mercy, then began chanting "hang, hang, hang!"

"Mr. Larson climb the god damn ladder now, or so help me; we will do it for you! Either way you are dying here today, I promise you that."

It was at that point; he had realized that his fate was now sealed. He looked around at the anger of everyone. And gave up. With a rope tied around his neck, and his hands in handcuffs, he began slowly climbing the latter. Which was extremely difficult with his hands now behind his back, in cuffs. Once he was at the second to the top run, I then asked, "Mr. Larson, do you have any final words you would like to say, before your punishment is handed down?"

"Yes, this place is pure hell, we should have never come here. I wonder how bad it's going to get in here after another couple of years. You are all going to hell just like me, you just wait and see, I'm finally going to be set free of this place once and for all." It was then, not showing any hesitation whatsoever, he kicked the latter out and jump, hoping to snap his neck from the four-foot drop, and getting it over quickly. There was a snap, as he fell the four feet. His body then forcefully snapping to a stop. He squirmed around for about a minute. Then his body went completely limp. Like that it was all over. None of us felt good about what had just happened, but we also knew that it had needed to happen. No one had said a thing. As soon as it was over. Everyone disbursed and headed back to the own condo. Most I would imagine would have a drink.

It was quite sobering witnessing someone hanging. Once they had, we then proceeded to cut him down. loaded up Mr. Larsons body, then we gathered Ms. Larsons body, and cleaned the bloody mess up where she had made as she had bled out from her injuries. Then we went and cremated both their bodies together.

The funny thing was if I'm being truthful, I actually didn't feel bad by what we had just done, but rather, in a sick sort of perverted way, I guess. I felt empowered by this. I also insured my leadership role here today. I had tested the people's loyalty towards me. I clearly let everyone know that I was the one that was in charge. It was sort of liberating. They knew that I would act if they do wrong!

CHAPTER EIGHTEEN:

"And It Just Continues On"

THIRTY-FIVE MONTHS IN:

    I thought that with Mr. Larsons hanging, I just might have a little less problems with everyone for a little while. But that wasn't the case at all. it seems like daily small fights were constantly breaking out. Everyone seems to be on edge these days. I would soon learn that the small fights breaking out, weren't my biggest problem at the moment, at this point in time. Much bigger problems were now on the horizon. Things were growing darker in unseen predicable ways.

    Dave had been looking for me. "Robert, we have a real problem on our hands, I need you to come with me at once. I have something serious to show you."

    I could see the distress on his face, "Well, what is it?"

    "Just wait I would rather just show you."

    He brought me to the fishponds, the tub growing the trout specifically. Half of them were now dead floating on the water surface. There must be a couple of hundred of them that were dead. I was completely shocked seeing this, "What the hell could have caused them to die in the first place? I was just here yesterday, and they looked just fine then!"

"I don't know for sure; they have been fed, oxygen levels in the water are good, the PH is good. The temperature of the water is good. I really don't have any idea what is now causing this to happen. We better gather up all the dead fish, giving the living ones a fighting chance. I really don't think that we should risk consume any of the dead fish, they may be deceased. And whatever killed them, could end up getting us sick, as well. We, better monitor the living ones. See if we loss anymore of them. Holly shit, this is a huge food source for us. We can't afford to lose them all like this, we better damn well figure this out in a real hurry, so we don't loss even more of them."

We sadly ended up throwing thousands of pounds of trout out. It broke my heart having to do that. We were going to keep an eye on the remainder of the living trout. Something was definitely serious was going on here, but whatever it was, it was certainly eluding us. After we had removed all the dead fish, we shockingly started noticing even more were looking sick, and were still dying on us. And we couldn't do anything to stop it from happening.

We were gravely concerned about this. We put fish antibiotics in the water just in case the fish have some kind of disease. If we end up losing all the trout. We have no way to replace them if they all end up perishing. This would be a fifth of are fish stock. In four other tanks. We were growing Blue Tilapia, salmon, catfish, and the Yellow Perch.

The fish in the other fish tanks currently still looked good, no sign of distress. Over the next couple of days, we were carefully monitoring the condition of the trout health. And every day even more were still dying on us. Four days after discovering the fish starting to die. The last of the trout had perished. A very sad, serious loss. We drained the tank, and cleaned it out, sterilized it, so hopefully we could grow more of the other fish with the available tank. We also changed out all the filters in all the tanks. We just couldn't take any additional chances.

We kept this from everyone for the moment. The last thing that we had wanted at this point is to start worrying everyone. This was quite a huge hit to us, but we still should be able to get by, but with all the mouths that we had to feed, we would need to start cutting back a little, to be on the safe side. We were going to cut back by at least a third of the fish allotment for each and every person in here. We knew that the people weren't going to be happy by this decision, but we really didn't have much of a choice. It is what it is.

As of late, fights have been breaking out. People want to get their hands on more food. Then yesterday sadly, one of these fights had resulted in the death of two of our citizens. It seems there was a small poker game going on, and instead of playing for money, they were actually playing for higher stakes, they all betting part of their daily food rations for an entire week. So, the stakes were rather high. One of the guys ended up completely losing his shit. He grew extremely angered by this. He had been drinking quite a bit for several hours, certainly drunk as this was going down. Leading up to that faithful moment. He started accusing the other two men of cheating. They just started laughing at him. Not even taking him seriously. This really had ended up setting him off. It's what he choose to do next that was a real shocker. It was at that point that he went over to the kitchen, and he then quickly grabbed a large knife, and then unexpectedly stabbed both the men several times, killing them both. They had been too drunk to fight him off or be able to get away. Then he started screaming, "No I'm taking your rations instead assholes, what do you think of that mother fuckers?" Happy with himself. His closes were covered in the men blood. He brutally stabbed them both many times each. It was about an hour later both their bodies had been discovered by one of the murdered guy's wife. When he hadn't returned home for dinner or answered her calls to him, from her. She grew curios and decided to come check on him.

    Then a search party for Mr. Williams was then conducted. Once everyone had heard about what had happen. He was trying to hide from all of us, it's not like there was any where that he could actually go, but we could follow his whereabouts on camera. Dave headed to the command center and started looking through the cameras to try and locate him. Within just a couple of minutes we had located his where abouts.

    I'm not going to lie, hearing we lost more people, I felt a small slight sense of relief from it, knowing that there was going to be less people to try and feed, after knowing we lost all those fish. I know that sounds warped, but that's just how it is. This senseless act was going to help us in the end. Think how much three grown men will in in two years, That's a lot of food.

In the end Mr. Williams, I think he had sobered up enough to have realized what he had just done and knew what we would do to him once we had caught up with him. He ended up slitting his own throat. He was in the bathroom in the pool shower at the time he had killed himself. He had the shower running. It was a good thing that he was because he had quickly bled out all over. Most of the blood had gone done the drain. So, there wasn't as much of a bloody mess that we had to clean up once we found him.

Once again, more have dead while we have been in here. We have had three people murdered, three commit suicide, and three die. Nine people This place is slowly killing us all off. Rotting our souls from inside out. Taking once good people and turning them into something so completely different then what they once were before coming here. Almost every day. We were paying a rather huge price by being survivors.

Maybe this was all karma, letting us all know that we weren't meant to survive the fate of what had happened on the outside. Maybe that was the reason, we have been slowly dying off. Just maybe that is the reason we are losing the fish, so we would all in the end, end up starving to death.

   I'm not immune to the physical, and mental effects of this place is taking on all of us. I certainly have thought about killing myself from time to time, so I wouldn't have to be tortured by this place for another day. Every morning when I wake up, I absolutely hate to have to face yet another long-drawn-out day of all this. Every day in here is the same.

   I really missed Cindy. It was so lonely not having her here with me. Every day is always the same fucking same thing over and over again. Just like that movie ground hog days. There is no more excitement here. Nothing to ever look forward to. The boredom is the worst enemy that we have to face in here. The day that the doors finally do end up opening up, is still a very long ways out. I think the only reason I haven't actually ended things, is because of my precious daughter. I can't possibly do that to her. Though I still don't have her living with me, the highlight of my day, however, is when I go visit with her. It's the only thing that I still look forward to each and every day. She really is the only joy that I still have left in my life these days.

I'm so sick of having to deal with all the problems of this place has to present to me. Everyone always seems to bitch at me. I would have never thought that I would have to deal with the people murdering one another. Or people killing themselves. Or the cheating lying and stealing that's been taking place here. The evil of each and every individual has been starting to surface, and manifest in strange new ways. I was so naïve what this place was going to do to us. If I would have known the truth. I wouldn't have gone through with this project. But back then, all I thought about, was just how much bloody money that I was going to make. I should have thought about the phycological effects such a stay would take on a person. I could have never envisioned that things would become that bad.

Now with the loss of so many fish it was a huge, worrisome hit on being able to provide enough protein in all our diets. I really hoped that we don't loss anymore of the other species of fish that we currently are now growing. If we did. We could be in real trouble. And we would surely end up all starving long before the doors open up again.

  We never figured out why all the trout had ended up perishing. We then shockingly started noticing the salmon were now looking sick as well. We were trying everything that we could, from preventing another fish kill off like we had with the trout. But two days after we noticed the first salmon starting to get sick just like the trout had. Some of the salmon had started perishing as well. And within just a weeks' time from the salmon starting to show signs of sickness. They had all died as well. In two weeks, we have lost upwards of 50% of all our entire fish stock. This could mean that we all are going to end up slowly starving. The only other protein that we had was the chickens, but we really couldn't start consuming them, because we needed them for their egg production at the moment.

  I decided it best to try and keep this from everyone in the community. We couldn't afford everyone starting to panicking not just yet. Though things were starting to grow much more dire, and bleak. After all we still have two years to still have to go. But they would be finding out soon enough, when they realize they aren't being given and salmon, or trout any longer.

CHAPTER NINETEEN:

"Food Cut Back"

FOURTY EIGHT MONTHS IN:

    Things really have gone from bad to much worse for us. We haven't lost any more fish. That's about the only good thing that's happened as of late. But the damage of losing the fish that we did, is already done. Something that we wouldn't be able to recover from. We surely won't be able to recover from before the doors finally do open up. We never did figure out what had caused the fish to die like they had. But even though we haven't had any more fish kills. Because we have been taking fish away to eat, faster than we can actually now reproduce them. I'm not sure how much longer that this can actually continue to go on before we actually end up completely outstrip our current supply. At which point we will be majorly screwed.

    But it's not just the fish supply that has now become critical, all our other supplies are slowly starting to run out as well. It would seem each week, that we have been running out of something else, something new. Whether it's from the freezer, or dry goods. It's all running low. And we still have so much time to still have to go, I really didn't know what to do.

As a result of this particular fact, people are getting quite angry, and much more verbal in nature. It's understandable, none of us have been getting enough to eat, not by a long shot. It really sucks being hungry after I just had eaten. The truth was none of us were getting enough to eat any longer. Now taking enough calories in daily. We were all losing quite a bit of weight as a result. As a result, all my clothing was quite loose on me now, and I don't have much energy. And my stomach growls all the time now.

As we all started slowly starving, the unthinkable was starting to happen. People were so desperate to get their hands on even more food than they had been given, just to keep from starving. That they have been now resorting to outright stealing from one another. But sometimes people have ended up dying as they were fighting to steal other people's food. All loyalty, and humanity was slowly being thrown out the windows. As the people grew very desperate just to be able to survive. Survival of the fittest was now heavily in play.

  No longer did we do any sort of community gatherings. It was becoming too dangerous for anything like that anymore. Everyone was arming themselves were ever they went now. You never had any idea if anyone was about to attack you. You can't trust anyone any longer. You always had to look over your shoulder just in case. The residents were as it turns, manufacturing weapons out of just about anything that they could get their hands on. Joe and I didn't let the kids leave the condo any longer. It was too dangerous. We feared if they did, the others would either kill them, or capture them and try and use them as pawns against us, and then to force us to give them more food.

  Dave, Joe, and I now don't go anywhere without our guns, strapped to us. We have the biggest targets on are backs. I personally have been attacked twice now, just in the last month. Once when someone wanted me to take them to the restricted area where the food is being grown. I sadly I had to end up shooting and killing one of my attackers. Most of the attacks on us, have come when we are handing out the provisions.

People who were dissatisfied with the amount of previsions that they were given for the next week. We used to personally deliver the rations to each and every condo. That has become much too dangerous for us now. Now we have the people all come to the great hall, at assigned times. And if they don't show up, at their assigned time. They will lose out altogether. One of us hands out the food, and the other two, stand guard, while they are holding their guns. Clearly visible to the others.

But then one of the most dangerous times for those that are picking up their own rations, is actually making it back safely back to their own condo safely with their food still in hand, can prove to be very dangerous for them. This is the time that people have been being attacked. Especially the older people amongst the population, that physically can't defend themselves as much. People like this have ended up being wounded, or even worse have been murdered, trying to fight their attackers off. People had to keep their own condos locked up at all times. Or their neighbors can try and break in.

The fact is, we have all descended into pure kayos, pure madness. It was now everyone for their selves. I can't believe what we have allowed ourselves to descended into. It's amazing what happens to you, as you slowly end up starving to death. It becomes to a point, that, food is all about which you can think about. And when your stomach is constantly growling. It's impossible to ignore. Nothing else matters.

  I was starting to grow gravely anxious. We are running out of food plain and simple. It was a fact that I was having a hard time coming to terms with. I thought I had perfectly planned all this out before we came here. Boy was I completely wrong about so much. The amount of food that we now still have available, I really don't think that we can hold out for another twelve months locked away in here like this. Not even close to that, with how many people that we are currently having to feed. Twelve months is how long we still have before the doors finally do open back up once more. We are all going to die long before that happens.

  Dave, Joe, and I went to the command center. We were growing quite worried, as our remaining food supplies was going much too quickly. At this current rate we realized that we only had less than three months' supply of food left.

That's when desperation makes you consider doing something so radical, in order to try and survive. One wouldn't normally consider such a drastic sinister thing even a month earlier. But this is where we now find ourselves.

We spent a couple of days going through our supplies, just to be sure we weren't perhaps wrong. With the amount of fruits, and vegetables we are growing. The amount of dry goods we still have left in storage, and the freezer were nearly now completely empty at this point. And we would need to ration out the fish as well as the chicken we still had left. Plain and simple put, between the loss of so many fish, and not being tight enough with the supplies in the first couple of years, that's how we got ourselves in this predicament in the first place.

The question now is, knowing all this, what the hell are we going to do to try and make it through the remainder of our time that we still have left. Do we ration out the food we still have left. Only to in the end to have all of us to starve to death within four months if we really stretched it out. Or do we sacrifice a number of us. To hopefully save the rest. None of us wanted to have to consider something as radical as this, however the truth is, we bother save some of us, rather than all of us having to end up perishing. Otherwise, all of this would have been for nothing. But we would all have to agree to something so sinister, but yet we were. We went back and forth for hours. In the end we all had agreed we had no other choice. He would have to do it.

Once we had decided this, we had to decide on exactly on how we were going to actually carry this out. How do we decide on who is going to live, and who is going to die. And then disposal of all the bodies. What gave us the right to do so. We convinced ourselves it was the right thing to be done.

Dave then had a disturbing suggestion, "We could shut and lock the door to tower six. There is 25 people living in that tower. So, they would be contained. Then we cut off the flow of fresh oxygen. Also cut off the water, and communication, and of course food. We estimate it would take at least three days for them to start perishing. We would be able to monitor the tower's going on, through the cameras. Then once they had perished, we could just leave them were they had died. I was not liking this idea at all. But as the leader. I knew it was better if I could sacrifice them to be able to hopefully save the rest of us. I gave the order to move forward with the plan. Don't think that I took this decision lightly, not by a long shot.

    We waited until the middle of the night. We had to be sure that all the tower residents were back in the tower before we did. Once we were sure of this, we locked down the tower. Then we shut off the oxygen, and water to the entire tower, and cut they ability to communicate with us. "Gentlemen may God forgive us. We may end up going straight to hell for this."

    Then we sat back and grueling watched the cameras. It was three hours before anyone from tower six had noticed that there was something now up, when they had tried to leave the tower. These cameras also had volume. They started screaming realizing that something was now definitely up. He went over to a nearby air vent and noticed there wasn't any fresh air now blowing out. If it were working, it would be. He then went to a need by water faucet, to see if there was any water, and he then discovered that the water was also shut off. It was Mr. Whitmore, he went to all the condo's telling everyone, that we had locked them all in. They clearly figured out what we were now doing to them. They tried desperately to open the door, but there would no physical way that they could open it.

   The first thing that had started to affect them, was not having any water at all to drink. Going without water was taking a real toll on all of them, two days in. There would be enough oxygen for a couple more days, but still that was slowly running out. And the carbon dioxide leaves was now drastically building. Then combined all this suffering with having no access to food. They were already going into this slightly slowly starving, before we had even locked them in. Which would speed the process up of dying.

   I think with the guilt of what we were now doing, we were glued to the cameras. Sort of like watching a train wreck. Three day's in, and none of them were still actively moving around any longer. They had grown much too weak for any exhaustion. The hardest thing was watching the children having to die, there was three children that lived in tower six. When I was by myself, I ended up bailing. This was absolutely tearing me up on the inside.

   None of the people in the tower, no longer had the strength to continue fighting on. They all were laying down at this point in time. Family members laid together, just waiting for the moment of their death to come, so they would no longer have to suffer. The children were the first to end up perishing. Three days after we locked them all in. I threw up as I observed the first child expiring. By the end of the third day, a total ten people had ended up dying. And by the four day, the oxygen levels were drastically getting low, and the levels of carbon dioxide were hovering at dangerously high levels. It was either the oxygen levels, or four days of not drinking water. The people in the tower's, organs began shutting down. By the fifth day we no longer detected any movement at all. They had all now sadly perished. I was relieved that they didn't have to suffer any longer.

Now with the horror of what we just did, I haven't slept more than a couple hours since we put this plan into action. When I did, I suffered from horrifying nightmares. I'm haunted by each and every one of their faces, I was drinking a lot as a result trying my best to stay numb. Funny we still had a lot of alcohol still left.

The day after we locked the doors to tower six. I had called a mandatory meeting for the remainder of the peoples, "I used the meeting to honestly explain how dire things now were for all of us. I explained what we had done to save the rest of us. Several people began to cry, both sad at all the people that were going to die, in order to save the rest of us, and the fact that things have gotten this bad. Joe, Dave, and I were shocked that everyone understood why we did what we had. Certainly, no one was clearly happy about what had to happen. Now we were all in this together, and now would be forced to live with our guilt in trying to save ourselves, at the price of others. What we had to do in order to survive. The mood amongst us was very somber. Upon hearing this, it had really taken the wind out of everyone's sails. But as much as they didn't want to have to admit it, they were relieved that it wasn't them locked in the tower.

CHAPTER TWENTY:

"Things Continue To Be Bad"

FIFTY-TWO MONTHS IN, EIGHT MONTHS TO GO:

Even though we had single handedly sacrificed twenty-five poor souls, in what now a purely to be a vain attempt to save ourselves. That being said, just because we did, we still find ourselves still desperately low on all are food supplies. All we had done really, is bought ourselves another couple of months at best. We still have eight long grueling months to still go. That still seems like an eternity.

The ugly truth of the manner was that we were falling far short in our attempt. Joe, Dave, and I had come to comprehend that we still have way to many people to still have to try and feed each day.

We seriously started talking about now shutting down tower number five. We currently have twenty people living in this tower, say we were to go through with this. This would get us down to just twenty-one people still left alive. If we did this, we just might finally have a good chance at actually making it the remainder eight months in here. Left with no other alternative, other than not doing it, and then all this was for not, and then we all end up dying if we don't go through with this. I wasn't willing to let that happen, so we reluctantly preceded to lock down tower five. Of course, doing this surely was going to get me a ticket straight to hell. Oh, who am I kidding, I already have earned that golden ticket. And what gives me the right to decide who will get to live, and who is going to die!

I couldn't end up constantly watching the camera's like before. Just watching, waiting for them to die all slowly. But I knew it needed to be done. If we didn't, we were all going to die. Our situation was much more dire, then when we had locked down tower six. We were growing sick from the more advance stages of starvation that's taken a powerful hold of us all.

Five days after locking down tower five, they were all now died. Most had died on day three, but there was a few hold outs. And the people that were still alive, didn't look much better than the ones that had died in tower five, from the concentration camp back in World War Two. I just hoped we were going to be able to pull through to the end. I honestly didn't know if we would. I have lost so much weight; I can now see all my ribs. And most of my other bones.

Starving has taken a super toll on all our overall general health. I have noticed another effect starvation has on the body, that was my hair was now starting to fall out in clumps.

My own dear daughter. She's six in a half, she has been barely able to physically get up on her own anymore. She currently weighs what a three-year-old would weigh. She has been getting so visibly weak, more so with each new passing day. I frankly have been so worried about her. I try to keep her entertained by letting her watch her favorite movies in bed. Trying to keep her mind off of food. Of course, that was impossible to do so. She ends up crying telling me how hungry she is. It absolutely breaks my heart not being able to do anything for her.

With twenty less people to now be forced to feed, I increased the amount of food that I was giving her, hoping to reverse the effects of starvation has had on her, and the rest of us. But it wasn't just her that was in pretty rough shape currently. Four other people had sadly succumbed to the effects of starvation since just yesterday unfortunately. With their deaths, there was sadly now just sixteen of us now still barely hanging on to life. Understand that We once had seventy-eight people. That's a whole lot of people to have lost. This little experiment of mine has those far gone bust.

   I tried increasing the amount of food that the remainder of us that were still breathing were receiving each day. Some of us were in pretty rough shape by this time. These are the people that needed to be taken care of. Over the next week, I choose to nearly double the amount of food each one of us were now receiving. I was desperate to save everyone that was still here alive amongst us. Dave and I began cooking for the others.

   Three more months had passed since the residents of tower five had perished. We now just had five months to go. So, I was very determined to build all our strength up. Prepare us for the day when we would all finally be able to ultimately leave this hell hole, once and for all. But what I would end up cruelly discovering, is that starvation is a funny beast. It can effect each one of us in much different ways. Some of us were more seriously sick than others. This list included my dear sweet daughter, my niece, and nephew, Joe, and Catherine, his wife. They all were the only family that I still have left in this cruel world. That drastically worried me. I really was doing everything that I could possibly do to try save them. But none of them were getting any better. I just really didn't understand why. I was attending to them night and day, by this point. My own strength was slowly returning, as I increased the amount of food I had been eating. My stomach wasn't growling all the time any longer. I needed my strength more than ever, to be able to physically care for my family, and anyone else still too weak to still get up. As many were still racked with sickness brought on by the effects of starvation. I had managed to put about ten pounds back on.

 Then sadly two weeks later, my own dear sweet niece, and nephew suddenly passed away, a day apart from one another. Their poor little bodies simply just couldn't take it any longer. They had both meant so much to me. I felt like my heart had been ripped right out of my chest.

 When Joe, and Catherine lost their children, it truly had devasting effected the both of them beyond belief, their own will to live, and continue to fight to survive, had completely vanished after that. Their hearts were completely broken. After their deaths, Both had begun refusing to eat any longer at that point. There was nothing that I could possibly do or say to either of them to change their minds. They no longer processed the will to live. I tried everything that I could to convince them otherwise. They had lost to much. They were already so sick, that they felt it would now be better to go join their children. And not have to suffer like this any longer.

None of this was important to them any longer. They no longer wanted to try and survive long enough for the doors to open again. Catherine perished just three days after her children. I don't think it was starvation that had outright killed her, but rather mostly a broken heart. By this point, Joe was in such bad state, that I wasn't even sure he knew that Catherine had died. He was pretty far gone. He was no longer responsive to me.

I stayed by my brother's and my daughter's side. I prepared myself for what I knew what was surely going to be coming next. I knew that at any moment now, I would end up losing Joe very soon. This was extremely hard to have to watch this happening to my dear sweet little brother. I didn't want him to have to die all alone. He truly is my best friend. He always has had my back. And I knew that this was all my fault. All this was my idea. I had dragged him all into this. He just agreed to go along with his big brothers' dreams. If it wasn't for me. They wouldn't have had to suffer like he is now.

It's what he wishes for, so it would be selfish of me now to not honor his last wish. I owe him, for all the horrible things I ended up putting him through. Joe breathing had become very labor intensive this morning, and over the next hour, each breath that he took, grew in length of time, in-between each breath. I knew it was his time to leave me. I wanted to say goodbye to him before it was too late to do so.

"Joe, I don't know if you can hear me or not, But you have to know that I love you, I'm so very sorry for bringing all this upon you, I hope you can find a way to hopefully forgive me. I know that I certainly don't deserve it. its ok Joe you don't need to fight on any longer. Go join your precious family!" I wasn't sure if he could hear me talking to him or not, but just moments later he took his very last breath. I cried for a long time afterwards. I felt so completely empty and lost on the inside. It hurt so bad. I eventually wiped my tears. Stood up and went into the bedroom were my daughter was currently. She was all I had left in this world now. I wrapped my daughter up in a blanket and picked my girls frail little body up. And held her in my arms. She was sound asleep at the time. I didn't want to wake her. I continued to softly cry. I was completely overwhelmed with emotions. I think I would have ended it right then and there, if it wasn't for my daughter, I was completely depressed.

   I didn't have the strength to do anything with their bodies at this point. So, I just locked the door to the condo as I had left. I brought my daughter back to my condo. And I then gently laid her in my own bed. I then laid down next to her. I gently held her little hand. I was so completely exhausted both physical, and mentally. I haven't had much sleep-in days. I had been staying up and caring for my family. I passed out from shear exhaustion, and I was completely emotionally, as well as physically drained. Hours later I woke to my daughter kissing my cheek. I looked over and she was smiling at me. She knew exactly what I had needed. It was the best medicine in the world.

Now there was just twelve of us that were still left alive. Losing so many. We certainly now without question, finally after nearly a year we had enough food to get through the remainder of our time we have left inside here. I drastically increase every one's food intake pure day. And over the next month. Everyone health was finally starting to slowly showing positive signs of improve. We just may have finally turned the corner. Everyone was starting to start once again putting on weight once more. I thought that this was very encouraging to say the least. I did everything possible to get everyone healthy once more. I had lost to many people on my watch already. I was bound and determined to not loss anymore. I owed that much to all the ones I have lost on my watch.

And over the next month, I didn't loss a single person. That was a really good feeling. As every one's health was now really improving. We all had lost so much already. We started looking out for one another. There was no more fighting amongst us, what was the point otherwise. We were all now determined to finally be free and rid ourselves of this horrible place, once and for all.

We all wanted to put this place behind us once and for all.

   As the time of the doors opening up soon. I couldn't but help and wonder what we would end up finding, as we finally find ourselves venturing outside once more, for the first time in five long hellish years inside this place. Would there be vegetation still alive, our any animals possibly still left alive, or any people that had survived the attack. Would the radiation be too high for us to be able to safely finally be able to leave this place behind. I really worried that the outside may be uninhibited.

CHAPTER TWENTY-ONE:

"Continued Problems"

FIFTY-EIGHT MONTHS IN, TWO TO GO:

Everyone included my own daughter had now almost fully now managed to have recovered for the most part anyways. We may never fully recover physiologically from all this.

I was starting to get really excited that we had just 61 days left until the big day finally comes. I know I was mentally preparing myself for this transition. But of course, it meant with the excitement of the approaching day, each one of the days we would be waiting drug out what would seem like an eternity. For every hour that pasted, felt like an entire day.

It was 2:16 am when my phone woke me up. My phone was alerting me of a problem in the command center. I quickly got up and rushed to the command center as quickly as I could. Dave had ended up beating me there. "Dave, have you figured out what's going on?"

"Well, it appears that we are getting low on water?"

"Is it the water pump? I sure hope not."

"I'm not quite sure! We better go down and find out what's going on. This has me really worried, I just hope that it's something simple!"

The two of us made it down to the pump room. It was clear instantly that there was something seriously wrong with the water pump. It was making a really loud clanging metal on metal noise, like grinding metal. I shut it down. We would have to tear it apart. See what was now going on with it. At this particular moment, this water pump was the most valuable piece of equipment that we have at this time. Because with the pump, we get all our drinking water, our oxygen, as well as heat, and in addition our power. Before we shut it off, we turned the gas generator on, so we could at least have power, and with the generator, we can produce oxygen, but without the water pump working, we will not have water, or heat available to us. Because our heat comes from hydroponic heating. Which requires a whole lot of water.

Dave and I worked feverously to try and rebuild the pump motor. But after nearly five years of constant running this equipment non-stop. We don't have very many spare parts still available to us. We were into the job several hours before we were ready to try and start it up once more. To our utter relief, our little band aide repair had ended up working. We got everything back up and running once more. I was relieved, this outcome could have been much worse. I knew that we were just really lucky this time around.

We checked to make sure all the systems were back up and fully running once more. One of the biggest things I was worried about at the moment was the current condition of the fish. Thank god they appeared to be just fine. If we would have lost them, we would have surely all been done for. Especially since we had previously eaten all the chickens. The fish were now our only protein source still available to us.

I headed back to the condo to be with my daughter. She was coloring at the kitchen table and watching cartoons. As I walked through the front door. She was so excited to see me and had come up and given me a great big hug. After what

I had just been through, her hug is exactly what I had needed.

I know that I was really hungry, I went ahead and made us both some dinner. It felt good to be a dad to her once more. It was because of her; I was given a purpose to wake up each and every morning. Otherwise, I fear I would have given up a very long time ago. Her personality was just like her mother. I get reminded of that each day. She looks so much like her mother. It was a shame that her grandparents weren't still alive, here with us. As far as family, it was just the two us still alive I'm afraid.

Conditions were finally much better for us. And we are so close now to getting out of the place. But you know the old saying when things seem to be too good to actually be true, then they generally are. Especially in our case.

Dave and mine repair didn't hold up for more than three days. The pump had shut off once more. The power had shut off, and the batteries had kicked in as soon as this had happened. I turned the generator back on. We had tried everything to get the pump back up and running once again. But it was toast, and this was already the backup pump. And the fact that we didn't have any more parts to try and rebuilding the motor again. Joe was the mechanic amongst us, and he was now gone. He probably could have surely gotten it running again, but sadly enough, he wasn't here amongst us. We kept trying to get it. With no luck whatsoever. With the generator, we had at least access to power and oxygen, but unfortunately, we now didn't have any heat, or running water without the water pump running. This was really worrisome.

So are greatest worry now was having access to drinking water. The one good thing is, when we knew that we were having troubles with the water pump. I had the foresight to think ahead just in case this was to end up happening again. All of us found any kind of container that we possibly could. And then we had filled whatever we could to store water in just in case this was to happen. So, we should be ok hopefully, but we really would have to ration the remainder of the water we did still have. To be able to carry us all the way through the remainder of the time that we still have left.

The one thing that was a real issue, what would we do with our human waste. We no longer had running toilets. We would have to use buckets to go the bathroom in, and when full we ended up dumping it in the swimming pool. Then the other thing that was a real problem was without the power pumping water. We didn't have any hydroponic heat. The facility was beginning to become really quite cold, as the concrete grew cold. We had to wear additional layers of clothing in order to try and stay warm. Each day the place was getting even colder.

   I was trying to try and remain positive through this for all of us. We had made it a month living under these horrible new conditions. But the water now was running critically low, we had to cut each of our daily rations of water down by 70%. So, none of us were really receiving even enough drinking water, but just enough to keep from dying. Not enough to bath or do our laundry. But if that wasn't bad enough. We no longer had any water to water any of the fruit trees and vegetables any longer, so they began slowly dying off. Cutting us off from another valuable food source.

   So, because of this we once again started slowly starving. It was hard facing this mess once again. This was a huge stressor on our health. This was pure madness. Once again after a month of this, more people started dying once more. Within a month of the water pump going tips up, five more people had died on us. And sadly enough, there was just seven of us now still left alive. I had a hard time wrapping my head around just how many of us have perished those far. I was feeling like a complete and total failure by this fact.

   I not sure why exactly, but I started suspecting that some of the bad things that have been happening around here, well just maybe have actually been happening because of sabotaged. I had to put my suspicions to rest. So, at night when everyone else was asleep, I began going back and reviewing the camera footage, night after night. I wasn't quite sure what exactly that I was actually looking for. Then after a week of doing this, I received my answer. It was like getting hit hard in the gut very unexpectedly. I just couldn't believe it, but there it was plain as day, on the camera. The camera doesn't lie. I caught my trusted friend Dave in the act of sabotaged. It had been him all along. I went back to the dates and looked at the fish kills. Oh my God that was him as well, he was poisoning them, It was all him. So many of us would still have been alive if it wouldn't have been for him. He had brought a lot of pain and suffering on to all of us, and as a result of his selfish actions, so many ended up dying as a result of his senseless act, including my own brother. I didn't understand why he would have gone and done something as sinister as all this. I felt pure rage now flowing through me. I knew that I was going to make him pay for what he has done to us all. Putting us all through hell like this, it was so senseless, and so tragic.

I wanted to find out exactly why. I decided I would confront him, but I would be well armed first. Dave had possessed a lot of specialized skilled he had learned why in the special forces, I would have to catch him completely off guard, while he wouldn't in fact being expecting it. Otherwise, I wouldn't have a chance to overtake him. So, I planned it out. And I certainly could let him know that I was now onto him. I needed the element of surprise.

I had convinced him that I wanted us to at least try and get the water pump up and running just one more time. About a half hour after we started to tear the motor apart one more time. I went to go retrieve a 3/16th open ended wrench from the toolbox, this had been my plan all along. Not paying attention to me, and his back turned towards me. I pulled out my gun and not hesitating. I shot him in the back of his left calf. He screamed out in pain, before he could even do anything to try and defend himself. I then shot him in his other leg. He was now powerless to stand or even physically try and getting away from me. I evened the playing field in an instant. He couldn't come for me now, but I could for him. He fell to the ground, screaming out in a great deal of pain. I went over and then kicked him hard in the gut. Then kicked him in the face. Then finally I started yelling at him, "I found out what you have been up to, you son of a bitch. Why in the fuck have you been trying to purposely kill us all, why would you do something like that. I fucking trusted you. It was all you, all along why?"

Dave even though in pain, laughed a bit, and spit blood out of his bleeding mouth before speaking, "Well the cat is out of the bag, I guess. You want to know why I did what I did, I'll tell you why asshole, because I enjoy killing, in fact I get off on it. It's like a drug to me. I didn't want anyone surviving, I just wanted you to all to believe that we were going to make it out of here alive. Seeing you all suffer and having a small measure of hope. It's like a powerful drug to me. You have been trusting the wrong man all along my friend, now haven't you. I had planned on you and me making it all the way to the end, and just as the doors opened up, and you thought that you had finally made it, I would shoot you, and then I would kill myself!"

"You're really fucking sick you know that?"

"I know that the funny thing was, you should have known that in the first place, before you started trusting me so much. I knew that once we were all locked up. I would have a chance to slowly kill everyone off. I had all this planned since the very first day we had come here."

"Tell me why in the fuck would you want to do that?"

"Because my government trained me to be a killer, and what I discovered not only was I pretty damn good at it, but I got off on taking life, and then one day I was told that I couldn't kill any longer. The military had made me retire. What kind of chicken sit was that I gave my life to the military, and they just had abandoned me.

Besides all these people in here, what gave them the right to have a chance at surviving, just because they all had so much ungodly amount of money and power. That shouldn't give them the right to survive over poorer people, not when everyone else had to parish. So, I therefore decided that I would be their judge and jury, for everyone that couldn't afford to buy their way into here. Furthermore, I wanted them to have to suffer before they had died. It wasn't fair that they got to come here in the first place. They have always lived the privileged life. And none of them knew what it was like to suffer, or being poor, so I figured starving would be humbling lesson on them. And you Robert, you're as guilty as they all are. You only built this place out of pure greed, nothing more. It was just a secondary benefit that you could retreat here as things turned to shit in the world.

    You know you're a real son of a bitch, do you realize that you never actually bothered to ever ask me about my own family. Don't you think that I would have wanted to save them here too. Oh, that's right, my family was poor, so they weren't welcome here. Just sucking up valuable resources. The only reason I was permitted to come here, was you needed me to help run this place. That's why I truly enjoyed watching you lose your own family, so you could feel what it was like for me losing my own. Of course, my job isn't quite done here just yet now is it. After me there is still six of you Basterds still amongst the living. Oh well there is still time for that to possible change, they just might end up starving first, hopefully your daughter doesn't make it. I really wanted to see you suffer some more! Especially after she passes, god it was hilarious how bad you had gotten when you lost your poor Cindy.

   It's funny really that no one noticed that I wasn't starving as much as the rest of you. You see I secretly stashed a whole lot of food away. I had to insure I was the last survivor. I generally go eat my stashed food. And watch the starving people in the cameras as I ate. It generally brings me great joy to watch the pain and suffering you would go through."

   Just then, unable to stay in control any longer. The anger reared up inside of me with pure unadulterated rage in me. Unlike anything that I had experienced before this point. I then went over to him. And began to physically beat him, with my bare hands. I beat him until I knew there was no question that he was dead or not. His face was barely recognizable by the time I was done with him. Then exhausted by what I had just done. I had beat on him for several minutes. I went and sat down on the ground. I had to catch my breath, any try and calm myself down. I was shacking uncontrollable. Though I hated him for what he did to all of us, and how he had gone about it. Truth be told, he was absolutely right about everything, as much as I didn't want to have to admit it to myself. It was all my fault once again; I created all this mess in the first place. I mean I had been so wrapped up in myself, I never even offered him a chance to bring his own family. Hell, it never even crossed my mind after all this time. And for that I am truly sorry, of course an apology is a little too late now, the damage has been done. And in doing so, I have become a horrible person. My own selfness had bought all this madness to our front doorstep.

 I just left him where he was. I cleaned myself up the best that I could, and then headed back up to be with my daughter. At this point, the only goodness left in me, was the love that I harbor for my daughter. Otherwise, this place has made me do some pretty horrific thing, transformed me. I knew there would be a point, that I would be answering for what I had done while inside here. I couldn't change the facts, what is done, is done at this point. And I have a lot of people's blood now stained on my own hands. Dave just happens to just be my latest victim of my own actions. Frankly, I have a difficult time looking at myself in the mirror any longer. I didn't like the person that stared back to me. This experiment has proved to be a complete failure. It had gone so completely wrong in so many ways.

   Yes, I knew that I certainly do deserve to die for my crimes, at least a hundred times over, but I had to at the very least, be there for my daughter at the moment. I wasn't sure what the world that I would be bringing her into, after we leave here finally. I had to prepare her, keep her safe, until she was big enough to be able to fend for herself. Then and only then, I should atone for my actions inside here. The list of crimes that I have perpetrated is going to be quite long indeed. There wasn't even a punishment big enough, or just enough for the crimes that I have heinously committed.

   I decided to put all this on the back burning just for now and see if I can save the five others that are still amongst the living. I need to try and make sure that they make it out of here alive at least.

Thirteen days was still a long ways to go, when we were basically completely out of food and water. These next days was going to really taxed us all quite fiercely.

   To bide are time, we did are best to conserve our energy. We all now stayed together to look after one another. I couldn't but help and wonder were Dave had stashed this food he spoke of. If I could find it, then just maybe we would have a chance. I spent a whole lot of time trying to find it. But I haven't run across any sign of it as of yet! I tore his place apart looking for it I looked everywhere in the command tower, no luck. Maybe he was just lying about that.

CHAPTER TWENTY-TWO:

"And Then The Doors Open"

FIVE DAY'S AND THIS WILL ALL FINALLY BE OVER:

   At this point, even though we are so bloody close to finally making it out of here, if I were a gambling man, I would bet against us at actually possibility of successfully making it out of here alive, our odds are very slim at this point. Why would I make such a bold negative statement as this, I'll tell you why, it's because we lost three more people. We lost them because We had run completely out of food and now just about out of water as well. We could only manage to have a couple very small sips a day. So, you can understand exactly why five days seems like an eternity to each one of us, at this point. The question is if we could hold on long enough.

   So, now it's just me, Ms. Wainwright, and my daughter that our still now alive, but we are only barely holding on at this point. We have moved ourselves to the entrance just inside the blast doors, so we would be ready when the time does end up coming. We were all not doing so good. We made ourselves beds right there on the floor, with in plain view of the countdown clock, and the doors. I didn't get up much. I was trying to conserve what little energy I still had left. In fact, we were sleeping a whole lot of the time now. There wasn't much else that we could do.

I woke up and happened to have glanced up at the countdown clock, I thought that perhaps my eyes were just playing tricks on me, so I rubbed my eyes. I then glanced back at the clock once again. The cloak said that we had five hours and twenty-two minutes. I suddenly got so excited! I then preceded to rolled over to see if Ms. Wainwright, was awake, so I could let her know the wonderful news. When she hadn't responded back to me. I rolled over to feel for a pulse. But she was cold to the touch. I would guess that she must had died several hours ago. I wasn't even surprised by this. It must have happened when I had been asleep. Dying of starvation is a very painful way to have to go.

Then I glance over at my daughter. Thankfully, she was still alive. I felt a real Si of relief wash over me. She was looking over at me. But she really didn't look so good. She didn't even lift her little head off of the pillow. I know that she really hadn't had the strength to do so. She was so frail now.

"Daddy, I have been laying here watching the cloak, We only have five hours, I'm so excited, Daddy could you tell me again what it's like out there."

I found it really hard to talk, my throat was so dry.

"Sure, thing honey!"

I did whatever I could do to keep her thoughts off of everything else. She eventually had fallen asleep. As she slept, I just stared up at the cloak. I started getting super excited. I could barely stand it any longer. We only now had five minutes until the big moment. I grew extremely anxious. I don't know why exactly but I was quite nervous. My heart started racing. "honey wake up, it's almost time now!"

"Really Daddy, I'm so excited!"

The clock moved from one minute, then began counting down in seconds. Suddenly I heard what had sounded like gears turning internally inside the elaborate locking mechanism. I couldn't believe it; it was finally really now happening. We had both been looking on in pure excitement. Five years I have waited for this very moment to arrive. There was so many times that I thought that I would never see this day arrive. I started crying in excitement. My emotions had caught up with me.

Then suddenly it finally was starting to happen, the doors were actually now slowly starting to open up all on their own, as they did, the natural light, and fresh air began to pour in through the opening all on their own. To be able to breathe in the fresh air for the first time in five long years was amazingly overwhelming to all my senses. Mixed in with all the freshness of the outside world. I had the gigger counter on hand, to make sure that the air was going to be safe for us to breathe. I took a few steps outside to check. It appeared to be just fine. Actually, I wasn't detecting any measurable amount of radiation at all. I sure thought that I would have. I was going to take this as a really good sign.

"Honey, would you like to go outside with me now? I know how you have been looking so forward to that. Daddy wants to show you the real world."

"Oh yes daddy, but could you please carry me! I don't think that I can get up."

I was really worried about her; I could detect it in her voice, in all the excitement of the moment, I had forgotten just how weak she was now. I knew that I was quickly losing her. In less there was a miracle, a way to save her. I didn't know what I could do to save her. I knew it was just about time, for my little angel to go to heaven. I could see the life in her slipping away rather quickly. I wanted to make her as comfortable as I could.

"Sure honey!" I went and scooped her up in my arms. She had lost so much weight; she was as light as a feather. And then the both of us excitedly headed on outside. It was so amazing to be outside once again. It was so bright out. It was nearly blinding. My eye's had to adjust. There wasn't a single cloud present in the visible sky around me. The sky was so blue. The colors were so much more vivid out here, more than I could ever remember. Having not observed this in so long, it was a true miracle indeed. There was a gentle warm breeze coming out of the north. I forgot how nice that was. All my senses seem to be coming to life once more, I really had forgotten just how much I had been missing out here, while being locked away. The smells that I was now smelling was so completely amazing!

The grass and weeds had become much overgrown since the last time I had been out here, even little trees were taking over the area. But then to my surprise, I heard the distinct sound of birds now chirping all around me. I could also detect the sounds of crickets. It was so pleasant listening to them. This was a rather pleasant surprise. There was also a gentle wind. It felt so good, the air was so completely fresh. Based upon what I'm now observing, there wasn't any measurable amount of nuclear fallout, out here. I was quite relieved to see this indeed. I thought that perhaps it had all been lost. Thankfully it wasn't. This was quite encouraging. I was thinking that the fall out, didn't reach all the way out.

"So, what do you think of this place honey?

"It's so beautiful daddy, just like you said it would be! But it's even prettier, and I can't believe all the new smells, sights, and colors. Thank you for sharing this with me now.

I noticed as she was saying this to me, that her voice was slowly now noticeably fading away. She was slipping away on me. And I knew that there was nothing that I could do to stop it now.

Daddy I'm tired, I'm just going to shut my eyes. Thanks, you for sharing this with me."

I tried to try and remain strong for her. "Honey I'm glad you like it. Honey, you have a good sleep now, go be with mommy now. I love you baby!"

Soon after I had said this, she smiled, "Good night daddy!"

"Good night sweetheart! You go to be with mommy!"

Her little head had then come to a rest on my right shoulder, and her body suddenly went completely limp. I began screaming out in pain. I began to cry when I realized that she had just passed away. I laid her gently down on the ground, after I had cleared out a nice spot with my foot, matting down the long grass. It wasn't fair, why couldn't she of all people have survived. She was so innocent and so sweet It just wasn't fair. Why in the hell did I have to be the only survivor, out of seventy-nine other people? This is not what I had wanted or had intended to happen. I sat down beside her body. I picked a wildflower and placed it in her hair. I thought at least she was able to see the outside world at least once before she had dead. So, her last memory would have been a happy one. I am a bit relieved of this. And I know that she didn't have to suffer any longer. She had tried so hard to be strong for me. And she never complained to me. I just think that she was just holding for me.

After a while, I just laid down beside her, I held her little hand. The sun felt so nice and warm. I stared up to the sky and enjoyed what I had missed out for so long. I would never take it for granite ever again. I had paid an incredible much too high of a price to see it once more.

Suddenly I was being haunted by all the poor people, including my family. Was my punishment for my crimes to spend the rest of my life all alone in this new world. Of course, if I couldn't get my hands on food and water, I wouldn't survive very much longer. Maybe a day or two at most.

CHAPTER TWENTY-THREE:

"The Outside World"

Lying down on the ground beside my dead daughter, I had fallen asleep in the hot warm afternoon sun. But when I ended up waking back up again, I was surprised to find that I was outside, and it was now dark out. It took me a moment to remember where I actually was. I was momentarily confused. One thing about starvation. It becomes hard to think, as the mind is being robbed of what it needs. Luckily for me, it was a warm night out. With a very clear sky, I stared up at all the stars. I had longed for this for so long. I started looking for all the different constellations I knew. I eventually fell back to sleep. As in my weakened state, I was drastically exhausted. As my body has been consuming itself, just to try and stay alive.

I woke back up as the sun was now just starting to slowly come up, over the nearby hills. The birds around me started to chirp with the arrival of the morning sun. I felt an urgency to now get up, but when I had stood up, only to quickly discover that I was extremely lightheaded, I in fact had almost passed out, trying to get to my feet. I really didn't feel so good. I managed to somehow stay on my feet. As it turns out. The sunrise on this morning was so beautiful, I had truly forgotten just how beautiful that they were. I would never take another for granite ever again. Being locked in there. I have grown to appreciate the small things that I had once taken completely for granite. I began to cry witnessing such a beautiful display painted across the morning sky. I was weighed down with so much guilt, that I was the only one of us that was now seeing this. The gravity, and guilt of the situation was hitting rather hard this morning. I missed my love ones so much.

   After I observed the sun rise. I knew I needed to get a move on this morning, and then try and get going before it had gotten to warm out. I was sad to just leave my daughter's body lying there in the grass all alone, but I had no way of burying her, I didn't possess a shovel, and I certainly didn't possess the strength to bury her. Besides she had spent most of her life underground. She was now free.

   I first had to try and get my hands on some food and water really soon. I was slipping away from the bounds of life. Then I had to try and figure out what's happened to the world in my long absences. I wondered if any of the cars here would even still start after sitting for so long, without being started up for so long. I went up to the first of the vehicles in the lot. It was locked. I moved on to the second one. The keys were left in the ignition, I tried turning it over. It was completely dead. I then preceded to check out every other vehicle that was present in the lot. They were either locked, which means I didn't have the keys, or the batteries were completely now dead from sitting for so long. Sadly, I had no luck with any of them.

    One of the vehicles I discovered had the skeleton of someone sitting in the driver seat, and then upon closer inspection, I happened to have noticed a handgun lying beside the body. I know longer remembered his name, but I bet this was the guy that had never made it inside in time. He probably couldn't handle being separated from his loving wife. I guess knowing the end of the world was coming in moments, he wanted to go out on his own terms. I would have probably done the very same things if the circumstances were the same. Oh god I missed Cindy.

Well using any of the vehicles was certainly out of the question at this point, so I was going to have to leave out of here on foot. Not such a grand idea when your currently starving to death, with death growing extremely close. Shit the gate to the place was currently locked. It had an electronic lock. I had to head back into the command room. Lordy I didn't want to ever go back inside again. I found the button and pressed it. I really hopped it had worked. Because the fence was electrified. I grabbed my blanket, and then decided to try and venture out of here once and for all. I never wanted to come back here ever again. Just the site of this place was haunting me.

The road into here, having not been used or maintained had grown in since I was last on it. I thought I would try and head into the nearest town which if I remember correctly was like a good thirty plus miles away. See if there is others still alive around here. If there were, then I could try and get some help. And I wouldn't have to be alone any longer. And I could get my hands on food.

It was quite a daunting walk to try and take on in my current physical state. The complex was situated high up in the hills. The sun was powerful hot by the time I was now planning on leaving. I think it was probably July, but I wasn't even sure of that anymore. Hell I didn't know what day of the week it was. I had to end up sitting down and resting several times along the way. I was so weak. I kept getting really dizzy. I had been walking now for hours when to my utter relief, I had spotted a large stream running along the road now fifty below me. I was so excited to be seeing this; I was dying of incredible thirst. My lips were all dried out and severally split. My mouth so dried out that couldn't even produce any more saliva. I had a really bad headache. And it was so warm out here. I hadn't been in this kind of heat in a very long time. So, I wasn't used to it at all. I was close to passing out. I think I now had a sunburn. My muscles ached really bad.

    Whatever I still had physically left in me, I began trying to make my way down the bank to the stream. I knew if I didn't, I would die within hours. The way down was loaded with loose rock, it was difficult getting a good foot hold, I ended up losing my footing, and tripping on my butt. I scrapped both my hands up as I had fallen. I slid down the hillside. I got back up and then made it to the bank of the stream. I put my head in the water. I then excitedly began drinking, oh my god it felt so good to finally be drinking water again. I wept because the water was so bloody good. I immediately felt the positive effects of the water was having on my body. I drank as much water as I could possibly stand. Making myself sightly sick, from drinking so much, and so fast. The water tasted so good, it had been so long since I had been able to bath, it had actually been months. There wasn't much of a current. And the water was only about four feet deep. Oh lord it was so good soaking. My muscles ached so badly. I stayed in the water for a great deal of time. Just for moment while I was in the water, I had forgotten about all my troubles. But then they all came flooding back in again. I was both physically and mentally completely wore out. I am so tired. Realizing that I was too weak to go on any further for the day. I set my blanket up there on the side of the stream, I got dressed and then laid down. I was so weak. Honestly, I wasn't sure that I could go on any longer. All that walking had taken a devasting toll on me. Once I had laid down. I really don't think that I had the strength to get back up again if I had wanted to. As much as I didn't want to admit it, but death was growing really close. I could now feel the life slipping away in me. This might actually be my last day alive on this planet. I was sure of that fact now.

   I was pretty sure that I wouldn't be able to physical go on, I realized that I was in fact now at my last stage of dying. And based upon how I was presently now feeling. I knew that death was rapidly now approaching. And there was nothing more that I could no longer do to stop it. I figured what was the point of even trying to carry on any further at this point in time. My family was all gone now. Everyone that I held dear to me.

   I figured this was as good as spot as any to go ahead and died. It was a beautiful enough spot. I laid down and stared out at my surroundings. At some point, I guess I had closed my eyes. At some point I would swear two angles were now hovering over me. My sight had become extremely blurry, I couldn't focus any longer. I thought it was time. I think that they were trying to say something to me, but I was too far out of it be this point, to make sense of what they were saying to me. And then I closed my eyes and surrendered myself to death.

CHAPTER-TWENTY-FOUR:

"The Hospital"

"Hey Jay let's try going up to the next bend, It looks like it might be a better spot to try and fish up there, because this area sucks. Let me go take a look first, I'll let you know. Why don't You stay here until I can take a look."

A couple of minutes later, Erin was calling out, more bloody screaming at the top of her lungs, to Jay being now about three hundred feet down the creek from her present location. Jay could hear the distress present in her voice. He knew something was seriously wrong. He dropped his fishing pole and came running to her aid.

"Oh my god, jay you need to come up here now, hurry up!"

Yelling back, "what is it?"

"Hurry just come here now, hurry!"

As Jay was approaching his wife Erin, he could now see why exactly she had been yelling for him. She was kneeled down in front of me. As her husband was approaching her.

"Jay, Oh my god, I feel a faint pulse. He's in some pretty rough shape, it looks like he's starving to death. Call 911!"

I briefly had opened my eyes, when I had heard talking, but I couldn't make out what the two angles hoovering above me. What they were saying to me, I passed out once more.

Jay had successfully called for help, on his cell phone, surprising that he had reception way out here. Jay patently waited up on the road above us, He was going to be watching for the first responders to show up. Erin had stayed with me.

"Don't worry Sir, we have help now on the way, you're going to be ok. Help will be here soon, you just hang in there for me, ok?" Of course, I wasn't responding back. Because by this point that I had passed out.

Jay saw an ambulance, fire engine, and a police car now quickly coming up the gravel road, at a great rate of speed. The dust was billowing up high into the air behind their vehicles. We could hear their sirens. They quickly pulled up by Jay, "Hey he's down there, my wife is with him now. He's in pretty rough shape. We have no idea who he is. We were just fishing, when we accidently had run into him just lying there on the ground.

The emergency workers grabbed their gear and then quickly began making their way down to me. They immediately began working on me, checking on my vitals. Then they put me on oxygen, and an IVE drip. They also looked for my ID, I of course I hadn't had any on me in five years. Then they carried me back up to the ambulance. And then rushed me to the hospital. I hadn't managed to wake up through all this going on.

I guess my situation was very critical, they really wasn't even sure at this point, if I was even going to make it. I was brought to the intensive care unit. I had slipped into a comma. I had been in my comma for over a week now. Meanwhile the Police were trying to figure out who I was. They checked in with my doctor every day to see if I had woken up. My prints weren't in the system. They wanted to be able to talk with me, to get some answers. They wanted to know who had done this to me.

When they had found me, most of my organs had been shutting down, and I had a high fever. After a week, I was still in a comma. In all likelihood, I would have perished the very day that I had been rescued.

At this point, the doctor was only giving me no more than about a 10 percent chance of pulling through this, and actually surviving is still touch and go.

Then thirteen days after I had been brought to the hospital, I miraculously slowly began opening up my eyes once more. I was freaked out, wondering where the hell I even was at the moment, or how did I get here. I hadn't remembered coming here. I then saw people walking around, outside my hospital room. So, there must have been others that had ended up surviving the nuclear attack after all. That was rather encouraging, knowing that I wouldn't have to all alone was comforting. I quickly found out that I wasn't unable to talk. I discovered that I had a tube presently down my throat at the moment. I just looked around trying to figure out what was now going on. I was really confused. I also discovered that at the moment that I was hooked up to machinery. I had an IVE hooked up to my right hand, and monitors stuck to my chest.

About a half an hour after I had woken up, there was a male nurse coming in to now checking in on me, having realized that I had woken up. he had immediately called the intensive care doctor on duty, to notify her of my improved condition. Moments later the doctor was coming into my room. She started checking on my vitals. And at the same time, she was saying, "I'm very glad to see you now awake, you're a very lucky man to even now be alive. You gave us all quite a scare. I'll tell you what, I'm going to pull the tube out of your throat. Now that you can breathe all on your own again. Now once I do this, your throat is going to be really sore for a while, so don't immediately try talking. Blink your eye's if you understand what I am saying to you."

I blinked my eyes, and she then proceeded to then slowly pulled the tube out, and then the nurse gave me a small sip of water.

My jaw was sore. As soon as I could manage to talk, I asked the doctor, "So how many of us had survived the attack? Because it's good to see others alive."

The doctor looked strangely back the nurse and me, "Can you tell me your name?"

"My name is Robert Hummel."

"Well Mr. Hummel, I'm not sure exactly what your even now talking about! Do you remember what had happened to you. You were severally starving to death when they had brought you to us. What had happened to you out there? Why where you starving. Did someone do this to you?"

"Please doctor, tell me how many of us had survived the attack, I really need to know. Did many end up surviving, I really hope so! Was it as bad as I imagined it was going to be?"

"Mr. Hummel, I'm not quite actually sure what your even talking now about! Will you please excuse me and the nurse for a moment."

They both walked out of the room, far enough away that I wouldn't hear them talking, "Nurse he truly is delusional, we better get Bob to come and talk with him. Could you give him a call?"

About a half an hour later, after looking at my charts, Bob had arrived in my room. "Well hello Mr. Hummel, My name is Doctor Watson, I am a phycologist on duty here at the hospital. Your doctor thought it would be good idea if you and I were to get a chance to talk. Would that be ok with you?"

"Sure, I guess so! I don't know why he thought that!"

"Very good than, your doctor had mentioned to me that you were asking him about, the attack, why don't you go ahead and tell me what you're talking about. Just so that I can understand more clearly."

"This isn't some sort of trick question. Jesus, Doctor, I'm talking about the thermos-nuclear attack from North Korea, China, and Russia five years ago. How many of us survived the attack?"

"Tell me Mr. Hummel, the events you speak of happened five years ago, could you go ahead and tell me where exactly you have been for the last five years, and how is it, that you came to nearly end up starving to death?"

"The company that I owned, built fallout shelter. I had transformed an old sixties missile silo complex into a luxurious bomb shelter."

"I see, so Robert, do you mind if I call you Robert?"

"Sure! Why not."

"So, Robert, is this were you have been, in your bomb shelter for the last five years?"

"Yes!"

"How long were you inside?"

"I, know we were in there 5 grueling hellish years."

"Wow! five years is really a long time? How many went inside with you to hide out?"

"There was seventy-eight others that had joined me."

"Wow that's a whole lot of people, your bomb shelter must be quite large to be able hold so many people at once. And for so long of a time period."

"Yes, it is!"

"So, Robert can I ask you where all the other seventy-eight other people are now."

"Oh, their all dead now, I'm the only one of us that ended up surviving!

"Oh my god, that's horrible, How did they all end up dying?"

"Oh, I don't really want to talk about that right now doctor. No, I don't want to talk about that. No, I can't! It's much too painful to think about! No, I just can't talk about that, please!"

"Ok Robert, we don't need to talk about that, right now. Ok for now, can I ask you what made you all decide to go hide out in your bomb shelter in the first place?"

You should know that answer to that doctor, we received the warning that the North Koreans, China, and Russia were preparing to fire off their nuclear missiles towards the United States. And we knew that the United states was going to do the same thing against them. So, we all quickly fled for the safety of the bomb shelter before any of the missiles had ended up striking the United States. And once we had all arrive and made it inside. The blast doors had then closed. And they couldn't be opened back up again for five years. That's how I arrived here. The doors had finally opened up after the five years was finally up, and I was finally able to leave. Wow you must have gone through a lot during the time while you were in there?"

"Yes, we all certainly did, but I don't want to talk about it right now please!"

"Sure Robert, we don't have to talk about it right now, maybe some other time."

"Doctor, I asked you a question earlier, how many of us had survived the attack? There couldn't have been to many."

"Robert, I now understand what you're talking about! This is going to be really difficult for you to hear all this. But you need to know the truth. Robert I could understand how scared you all must have been in the moment; trust me we all were at the time. Fortunately for the world, as it turns out, it was some Russian hackers that were attempting to try to start World War Three. They wanted Putin to annihilate Russia's enemies. Thank god all the countries involved had kept their senses with this, and each country quickly had thankfully stood down. So not a single missile was ever fired. Cool heads prevailed at the end of that day. The world was saved on that day. After that, each of the involved countries, had to agree to install some new safety protocols so this couldn't ever happen again."

"What are your saying doctor, that it never ended up happening? That can't be true!"

"Yes, in your case, that is exactly what I am saying to you. I'm sorry to have to tell you the truth."

"Holly shit! All that was for absolutely for nothing, so what you're saying to me, I gave five years of my life up for absolutely nothing at all. You mean to tell me, that I have lost everything, all because of a false alarm. I suffered so much for nothing. Doctor, I lost my family. How quickly was it found out it wasn't real?"

"No more than two hours, I think."

"You know what that means doctor, Dave would have had to have found this out, the truth, and not told me, or the others. He rather choses to lie to us. He must have wanted to trick us to go inside with him. He tricked us on purpose from the sound of it. It was him that locked the doors. Once those god damn doors had shut, we were all trapped in there like rats. There was no way to open them back up again, for five full years. He tricked us alright. No, no, no. It's not fair I tell you. How could he have done this to all of us. You know he wanted to kill us; he told me as much, well before. No, no I lost everything, thanks to that fucking bastard. No, I just don't understand how he could have done that to all of us."

It was at this point, that I began to completely loose it. It had proved to be too much to believe. I was now suffering a mental break down. I started screaming out in pure anger. I tried ripping my monitories off and was going to try getting up out of this bed, and then leave this place. I was being lied to by someone. The doctor quickly had sedated me. The effects of drugs worked quickly on me.

   While I was out of it, and my physical condition had improved enough, I was moved up to the nineth floor, which was the psychological ward. It was clear that I had needed some help. Mentally at this point I had completely lost it. Who wouldn't if you had just found out the last five years of your life was a completely a deceptive lie, and for this lie you had to give up everything that you held dear to you.

CHAPTER TWENTY-FIVE:

"Psych Ward"

Once the authorities had my name, they then began investigating much deeper of who exactly I really was. They quickly were then able to track down the bomb shelter. Then they headed out to the site to have a look around. They needed answers, especially if seventy-eight others in fact hadn't ended up making it. They needed to find out who exactly they were, and what had happened to them.

Once they had discovered the scale of what they had there. Being a small police department, they didn't have the kind of resources for this. The police chief had called in the FBI for assistance. At which time the FBI had taken over the entire investigation.

Within a day, they had their mobile crime lab rolled out on site, along with 15 investigators. They were going to investigate every square inch of the place. They were searching for answers. There was a whole lot of carnage to have to investigate.

Meanwhile, I had become completely delusional. Then finally my new drugs started leveling me out of it. I was making no sense to whatsoever. I was still too weak to be able to get up out of bed all on my own. I was slowly putting on weight. But some of my organs had possibly suffered permanent damage as of a result of long-term exposure to starvation.

Two FBI agents had ended up showing up to the hospital. A couple of days after I had been admitted to the psych ward. They both came and visited with Doctor Watson, asking for permission to question me. They had a court order to do so. They were there to hopefully to personally interview me. Based upon what they have been turning up with their investigation those far. They had a whole lot of questions for me, since I was the only survivor of this massive tragedy. They questioned why the person that had built the complex, turned out to be the only survivor. That was quite curious. It made me look a whole lot guilty, to say the least.

"Doctor Watson, we need to question Mr. Hummel about what he was involved with. It's vital that we personally speak with him at once. Is he mentally cognitive enough fit to be able to do so? This is very time sensitive. Can you allow us to speak with him?"

"The medications I currently have him on should allow him to speak with you. Now understand that the medicine is going to make him a bit lethargic, but as his Doctor I will need to be present in the interview, just in case, and if this causing him to much stress, I will end this interview immediately. Is this understood agents? Understand if we aren't careful, he could end up experiencing an extreme mental break down, if this happens, no matter how badly you want to talk to him. You won't be able to."

"Absolutely Doctor we completely understand."

"Ok, why don't you agents wait here in my office, While I go to have him brought here. This will take a couple of minutes."

While I was being prepared to be brought down. The agents had prepared for my interview. They had set up a camera, so they could record the interview.

A couple minutes later I was being wheeled in, in a wheelchair. I was currently too weak to be able to stand up or walk. I still had months of painful recovery ahead of me.

"Good afternoon Mr. Hummel, I'm agent Richardson, and this is agent Robey, we are with the FBI. We are here investigating the tragic loss at your nuclear bomb shelter. Would it be ok with you if we go ahead and ask you some questions here today?"

"Sure, I guess so!"

"Now just so you understand Mr. Hummel, I will be recording our conversation here today. So, what I would like to do is ask you a serios of questions, I would like you to answer my questions truthfully, and in as much details as you can recall, alright Mr. Hummel, do you understand?

"Sure, I guess so."

"Very good then, shall we begin then? My name is Agent Richardson, I am with the FBI, and my partner sitting to my right is Agent Robey. Today's date is July 18, 2027. Current time is 2:32 pm. We are here to interview Robert Hummel the lone survive of the bomb shelter were 78 others had perished. Ok Mr. Hummel, could you go ahead and tell us about the events that had lead up to you ultimately taking shelter in your bomb shelter."

"It was a Saturday; I don't remember the date any longer. I was sitting in my Livingroom, and watching TV, drinking coffee at the time. I was watching news stories on different events currently taking place, like the Chinese build up with their military near Taiwan, on the mainland. And the Russian and Ukraine war. As well as new saber railing from North Korea. These events had me quite concerned at the time. When my phone began suddenly going off. I had hoped that this day would never arrive. Because if this was going off, "things were going to hell in a hand basket," There was an app that my company had supplied everyone that had bought a condo in the shelter. There was two purposes to the apps. One to be able to keep track of the owner's whereabouts, and to be able to send a warning out to all owners, to come to the shelter at once. Because of impending doom, thermos-nuclear war would certainly classify as that.

The warning was sent out to all of us. I told my wife and daughter that we needed to go right now; I called my brother Joe. We went and picked him and his family up. And then we quickly rushed to the Skagit airport as quickly as we could. Cindy called her parents to make sure that they were coming. An hour in a half later we were pulling up in front of the complex. We grabbed are belonging and the hastily rushed on inside. It was an odd feeling knowing what we were now preparing to now do. I put my stuff down and turned back to take on last good look for myself, knowing it was going to be a whole long time before I saw all this again. And We had no idea what this was going to all look in five years, after a thermos- nuclear war has occurred. I knew that this was tearing me all up knowing that this was all really happening. I felt a slight sense of relief that we were going to at least be safe."

"Mr. Hummel, how many of you were there that day to take shelter along with you?"

"There was seventy-five, there would have been one more, but the poor guy didn't make it inside in time before the doors had automatically closed. His wife had barely made it in the nice of time. She would have been better off if she hadn't. She was the last person to make it inside. You know after the doors finally opened up again. I found the poor fellow, his remains were in his car, it looked like he had ended up shooting himself. Probably shortly after he was looked out, knowing they wouldn't open again."

"Wait Mr. Hummel, according to your doctors' notes, you told him there was a total of seventy-eight people?"

"Not on that day, we had three babies born while we were inside about a year on into our stay."

"Oh, I see, Mr. Hummel, who was the one that had programmed the blast doors to close and automatically lock up, for five years?"

"Oh, that was that son of a bitch Dave, my security guy?"

"Why did you call him a son-of-a-bitch?"

"Because I tell you why, I found out he had found out that it was all just a false alarm, he had to have found out before the doors were closed, that there was no missile attack. He could have stopped it, but rather for some strange enough reason, only known to him, he had lied to us all. Keeping the truth from us. Yet he for some reason still chose to lock us all in that hell hole!"

"Mr. Hummel, when did you end up finding out the truth what Dave had ended up doing?"

"Just recently, it when Doctor Watson told me that there was no missile attack. Then I had figured it out. That it had to be Dave behind all this."

"I see, Five years was a very long time to be locked up, that must have been extremely hard to have to face being locked up like that, and for so long. And not knowing what had actually transpired on the outside world."

"It was pure hell on all of us. I was so naïve what it was going to be like. It wasn't anything like I had envisioned it was going to be. At first it was for the first couple of months."

"How did you managed to get through it?"

"Well one thing is that I tried keeping myself busy and took my leadership role rather seriously. Everyone had counted on me. Every day I would go look at that damn countdown clock. Longing for the final day in there to arrive."

Mr. Hummel, I know that this maybe painful for you to have to talk about, but could you, please tell us how your wife had ended up dying?"

"I really don't feel comfortable talking about this, no I can't."

"Mr. Hummel, I'm sorry this is painful for you to talk about, but this could actually really be able to help me close my investigation quicker."

I turned and looked over at my doctor for guidance.

"It's ok Robert, it will be good for you to revisit these tragedies. By talking about it, you will start feeling better, and begin to be able to start healing. Don't worry, I will be right here monitoring you."

"How did your wife end up dying?"

"My dear, sweet Cindy died during childbirth, along with are second baby. While we were locked up inside. If we would have had a doctor there, inside with us, I sure that I could have saved the both of them. I was absolutely crushed after losing her. It was then that I couldn't bare being locked up in there any longer. She always had a way of calming me."

"What would you say was your mental state after losing your wife and child."

"I was so lonely; I really had a very hard time getting through it. After that I would say that I had started drinking a whole lot. I had to let my brother, and his wife raise my daughter for a while. I just wasn't able to be the father to my daughter for a good long time afterwards."

"Tell me Mr. Hummel, my partner and I need to know how all the others end up dying?"

Upon being asked that, I went dead silent. Just hearing that made me sick to my stomach, just having to think about all this all over again. I just stared down at the table. It was so painful to have to even have to relive those painful memories over again. When I have been trying to bury them deep inside. "I really can't talk about this. Doctor Watson I can't do this anymore. Can I please just go back to my room now?"

"Agents, I don't think that we should push this interview anymore today. I'm sorry to be cutting it short like this!"

Both agents look very frustrated by this sudden change of events. They needed to get a whole lot more answers out of me. And since I was the only one left alive. They had a whole lot more questions for me. I definingly was a possible suspect.

After I was back in my room, the agents went to go talk with Doctor Watson. They wanted to know exactly what my current mental state was presently. And exactly how far that they can push it with Me, because they had a whole lot more questions awaiting for me.

"Agents, please understand that Mr. Hummel has experienced a whole lot of trauma. I think that if we can take it slowly with him, we should be ok to try again tomorrow. You need to get him to start trusting you. If he doesn't feel threatened by you. He might begin to open up to you. Try taking it slow with him. I understand how important this investigation is to the FBI. I know with this many deaths, this is a daunting task for the FBI. I will do whatever I can do to try to assist you. Why don't we try again tomorrow, say around 10 am.

"Yes, Doctor that will work for us."

"Say agent, do you think that he killed all those people?"

"Mr. Hummel is our prime suspect at the moment."

"I will do whatever I can agents to get Mr. Hummel ready for tomorrow's interview.

Meanwhile, the agents headed back out to the investigation site, They considered necessary to catch up on any new evidence that had cropped up in their absence. So that they could figure out the line of questioning for tomorrow interrogation with me. They also spent a couple hours walking through the entire complex, to try and get a real feel for what it must have been like for us while I and the rest of us while were locked inside.

Over the last several days, the bodies have been being painstakingly removed, so that autopsy could be conducted. And the bodies could be formally identified, and then released back to the families for burials. Of course, they realized there was several bodies that were missing. Realizing the bodies must had been cremated.

The FBI was trying to maintain a media blackout on all this. At least until their investigation had been concluded. The other thing that was complicating matters for us, was the fact that everyone that had died, was in the top one percent of wealth in the United States. And their families had a lot of power, and clout, and knew some very powerful people in the top runs of the government. That would include the current President of the United States, and the Director of the FBI, and several people in Congress. So, the importance of this investigation was moved to the top of the burner. The deceased family members were demanding answers as soon as possible. So, they were keeping the pressure on the investigation.

   The next day I was brought in once more to answer more of the agent's questions. I was wheeled into the same room as yesterday. I noticed the same agents were here again. I was relieved by that.

   "Thank you for coming here again today Mr. Hummel. We will be recording this once again. Now just try to answer the questions the best as you can and be as truthful as you can with you answers."

   Agent Robey is going to take the lead today. Mr. Hummel, may we start calling you Robert?"

   "Sure, why not!"

   "Ok Robert, I would like to continue on where we had left off yesterday. I understand how difficult that this must be for you to talk about with us, but we need to find out what ever you can do. When exactly did you notice things starting to go serious wrong for you?"

    "There was many problems before this of course, including some suicides, but it was when we started to loss the trout, and salmon, a vital food source for us. Which only left us two other species of fish left. To try and keep ourselves feed. They started dying off. You need to understand this was one of our main sources of food, that we had for our protein. This was when things really seriously started going badly wrong for all of us. We quickly realized that we didn't have enough food to feed us all any longer. And be able to still make it to the end date alive. Not by a long shot. We began to all cut back on the amount of food that we allocated for each individual person. We had cut our rations in half. Over time we all slowly started to starve very slowly. We quickly had realized that this wasn't the answer. The thing that you have to try and comprehend detective, when a person is starving, it changes your personality rather drastically. It sort of rewires your brain. Food is all you can possibly think about, and any little thing can set you off. The need to survive becomes your driving force, and the humanity deep inside you, gets eroded away."

    "I see, so when did the first people start dying, and did they die from starving?"

"Well, my brother Joe, Dave and I realizing how much food that we still had available to us, and how long we still have left to still go before the doors would actually be opening up again. We checked several times, just to be sure that we may be wrong. That is if we didn't take some kind of drastic measures, we would all end up surely starving to death, We had lost a couple of people already from the effects of starvation. So, we decided that the only thing that we could do at this point, is to make a rather drastic move, we needed to sacrifice all the residences from Tower one, to give the rest of us a real chance at possibly surviving through this."

"Robert How exactly did you choose who would die? And who would live. That must have been a very difficult decision to have to make."

"Well, we had needed to eliminate about a third of our population we had figured, so we thought it would just be easiest if we just locked tower one completely down, so they couldn't escape, and then we cut them off from fresh oxygen, and drinking water, as well as food. Then once they had died, we just left them locked away inside the tower, so we didn't have to dispose of the bodies afterwards. The unfortunate thing about us doing this, was that they didn't end up perishing quickly. It took about five long grueling days for them to die all finally. It was miserable having to watch them suffer so much before dying."

"Robert how did that make the three of you feel after you had killed them?"

"It broke our hearts to have to witness such a spectacle tragedy that we had directly caused, Having to even choosing to have to do this was absolutely horrifying, but to not sound cold, it was also a huge relief much less of a burden to me, not to have to continue to be burdened to have to feed as many people as we had been. I wasn't sleeping much worrying how exactly we were going to be able to feed everyone beforehand."

"That must have been really tough on your all, knowing what you had done to those poor people, in order that you could survive? How many had ended up dying in tower one?"

I couldn't look either agent straight in the face at the moment, I was completely ashamed of what we had done to all of them. I knew it must sound really horrible to them, what I had done. I knew that I would have to live with it. I began to cry. Doctor Watson asked me if I was ok, and If I was good enough to continue on.

I wiped my tears from my eyes, and then responded "yes. I just needed a moment, to gather myself."

"Ok so after the people in tower one all had perished; did things get better for you all?"

"I believe there was 21 or 22 that died in tower one, my memory isn't so good on these meds that they now currently now have me on. Only for a short time things did in fact improve. But it started getting worse once again. And starvation started setting back in once more, so we were faced with making another painful difficult decision like before. We then had to sacrifice everyone then from tower two. The weird thing strangely enough, for at least me, was this time when we put tower two down. It surprisingly was becoming much more automatic, less personal, less attached to the people that I was putting down as before, with tower one. The only thing that was now mattering at that point was survival. We were becoming shells of our former selves. I didn't recognize the person that started back at me in the mirror. I didn't like the person staring back at me. I hated this person. Enough so that on more than one occasion I thought about killing myself."

"So, Robert how many of you were left after the people in tower two had ended up perishing?"

"I'm not exactly sure exactly, I want to say around twenty I think."

"Robert, so what happened to you the remainder of you next?"

"The worst possible thing had occurred to us, we started having problems with our water pump, which was already our back up pump. The pump was vital to our very survival. The pump supplied all are fresh drinking water. Provide the water for our heat, power, as well as oxygen, and our septic. Knowing that we may have additional problem with the pump in the near future. We began storing water in any container that we could possibly find. Sadly, for us all, about a week after Dave and I had tried rebuilt the pump motor, it had ended up completely crapping out on us, and we were unable to get it running again. It would have helped if we had new parts available. We didn't and we had to rob off the first pump to rebuild the motor the last time. We could rely on the propane generator for our electricity, and oxygen, but thanks to losing the water pump, we no longer had any water being produced, or heat. The heat was from hydroponics, and we were no longer able to use the toilets.

After this had happened, whatever water we had, we had to use strictly for only drinking. And we as a result of our critical water situation. So, we then ended up losing all the vegetables, and fruits that we had been growing. A huge food sources for us had been completely taken from us. I feared that this was going to be a death sentence for all of us. And we still had a couple of months before the doors would be opening up once more. This at that moment had seemed like an eternity.

Then we had managed to consume all our chickens. So, now the only thing that we had left to still eat were the fish. We were completely out of all the food that we had stored. We were all starting to die off from starvation. Each day we all grew weaker, and weaker. At that point in time, it was a question if any of us could survive long enough for the doors to open up again. It wasn't looking so promising any more. And more of us continued to die, including my brother and his family.

By the time the doors did finally open up, we had been completely out of water, and fish. I myself hadn't had anything to drink in two days and hadn't eaten in a solid week. My daughter and I were the only ones that were left alive by this point, when those doors thankfully had opened. My poor daughter was barely alive by this point. I knew no matter what I did at this point, she wouldn't make it, not even through the day. She had managed to have survived just long enough to at least see the outside world for about a half hour. It had meant the world to her. Before her than passing on. Losing her was the single worst thing happening to me. I was riddled with guilt for being the only survivor."

It was at this point that I started to ball.

Doctor Watson interjected, "Agents, I think that's enough for the day, don't you think?"

I was taken back to my room.

CHAPTER TWENTY-SIX:
"The Conclusion"

It had been a more than a week since the two FBI agents had last been here to speak with me. But they had returned once more. After having a private and long lengthy conversation privately with Doctor Watson, about me. I was being brought back to the doctor's office once more to visit with the two agents that had questioned me before.

"Robert in are absences, we have surprisingly discovered quite a bit about you, and what had actually happened while you were locked up in there. Things about you while you were all locked up in fact. The picture of what really ended up happening is a much different picture, than the one that you had painted for us. So, let's cut the formalities, and pleasantries. It would seem Robert, you weren't quite as truthful with us as you lead us, now were you. You know exactly what I'm talking about, don't you. You see it took us a while, but what you may not have known was that the camera's that were everywhere. Recorded absolutely everything, including the volume, 24 hours a day. Even inside the condos. It would seem something Dave had secretly installed. Everything was recorded for the last five years. It's clear just by the expression now present on your face, oh my god, Robert, you had no idea that the camera's had done this now did you? Your security guy Dave had installed the program. He must have got off by watching the residents inside their condo's. I wondered if he had watched your wife. Oh, I would imagine that he probably had. I bet that you had know idea about the camera's located inside the condo's, they were state-of-the-art, tiny, and very well hidden. Obviously if you hadn't known about them.

It took our tech agents awhile to crack his security measures. Or if you had known the truth about the camera's, I think you may not have done what you had done so openly. Or at least destroyed the recordings, they are quite damming against you.

Are people have been pouring over. Oh, we also found your journals, boy did they tell us a lot of fascinating thing, they turned out to be very enlightening. Let's just say that we have learned a whole lot of truth about you, and who you really are. So today we are going to change things up.

Rather than us asking you questions, no rather, we are going to tell you a true story, not the fairytale you spouted off to us, wasting our time. We won't be wasting your time like that. I'm sure, a rather familiar one to you. So, Robert why don't you go ahead and just sit back and just listen to us. You can correct me if I get any of the events wrong.

So, the first part of your story was correct enough. We had found Dave had found out that it had all been a false alarm. Yet he had still preceded to lie about it and went ahead and moved forward with the original plan. I guess none of us shall never know why exactly he had done what he had done. If he hadn't, then I really strongly think none of this would have come to pass. And seventy-eight people would still very much be alive.

According to your personal journal that you kept. Oh yes, we found them alright. I bet you wish we wouldn't have. I'm really surprised you hadn't. I know that I certainly would have. You had an entry for every day that you were in there. Our investigators are very thorough. The FBI won't stop until we know everything about you.

You were going out of your mind being in there. Your wife didn't know that you were Bipolar, did she? At least not until once you were locked up inside. That was your casteless dance. You wrote it was growing extremely hard to hid it from her. Well, it doesn't really matter.

About nine months in, you were finding your medication wasn't helping much, if not any. Less so with each new passing day. The stressors of being locked up was making it impossible to hide from the others.

You started finding yourself getting very irritated by how snobby all the owners had turned out to be towards you. Their true nature was coming out. That according to you included Cindy's parents. After a while they began looking down on you, treating you more as an employee, rather than an equal, like one of them. You thought how dare they when you have saved them all. You grew extremely upset that they didn't show their gratitude, for all that you had done to them. This was really rubbing you the wrong way. You grew extremely irritated by this. And you weren't going to let them get away with it. You wanted them to all know as long as they were inside, that you ruled over them, and they would need to be put in their place, and obey you're orders. It was at that point that you had decided to begin to get your revenge on all those that were treating you so poorly. And you slowly started demonstrating your absolute control, now didn't you Robert. You felt that it was extremely important that they respected you. And for those that didn't well you would make them end up paying for it. The stress of the place was really taking a huge toll on your sanity.

But it was about a year being inside after you had sentenced a man to death for killing his wife. Why didn't you just lock him up. Your wife became absolutely furious with you. She said that you had no right to do that. She hated you for going through with it, didn't she. She could see the truth of what was starting to happen to you. She had figured out the truth. She could see that you were mentally changing. A couple days after you hung that man. You seriously beat a man for coming up to you and complaining to you. It was becoming clear that you wouldn't tolerate any decent whatsoever, from anyone, including your own wife.

You were really growing to hate it in there, so the only thing you had was a lust for unadulterated power, and obedience from everyone, without question. Everyone could clearly see what you were becoming, especially your own wife. You hated her for the way that she now looked and started speaking to you. You both started fighting a lot after that. Now didn't you. You had a major blow up the very night she went into labor. You grew to really resent her. Especially since she wouldn't have anything to do with you any longer. You both had been sleeping in separate rooms for several months. You accused her of the baby not even being yours. This made you really recent her, so much so you ended up flying into a rage, and you ultimately ended up chocking her to death, with your bare hands. Didn't you, which had also ended up killing your unborn baby in doing so. Guess what Robert, we did a DNA test. The baby it was in fact yours, it was a boy. I thought you should know.

You wrote in your journal that you were hearing voices at this point. That they told you to eliminate her, and her parents. So, you did precisely that night didn't you. Shortly after killing her, you shot both her parents in cold blood. Right after killing them, you began to laugh.

So, the first thing that you proceeded to do after your wife's death, was you start killing the fish off. You had decided that you were slowly going to starve all of them into submission. You were going to show them. But that wasn't good enough for you now was it. Your Brother was on to you. He knew that your medicine wasn't working any longer. Once you figured out that he was onto you. You secretly locked him and his family up into their condo one night, while they were all asleep. You went to the command center, and then you cut off their air. Your brother begged for you to turn the air back on. Instead, you just laughed loud in the loudspeaker, so he could hear you. You wanted to be sure that he had heard you on to him. The voices you were hearing were telling you, your brother was a trader, and he was planning on taking you out. So, you wanted to strike first. They eventually ran out of oxygen, and ended up perishing, as you watched on in utter delight, thanks to you. You wrote in your journal how exciting it was to kill them. You demonstrated no remorse whatsoever. Then after Joe and his family's death, you wanted to put down any dissension that was still left.

Dave was on to you killing your brother, You knew he wanted to try and stop you. He was gravely concerned about your mental stability by this point. Truthfully everyone was. Everyone knew that you were completely off your rockers.

You knew with Dave's special force training he would get the jump on you, so you managed to catch him off guard, and then shot him in each legs, and then you then preceded to beat him to death. Then you put all opposition down. Now you could freely take your revenge that you so lusted for. And there was no one left that was strong enough, that could stop you any longer. You were now the only one that had access to the command wing and were all are food was. You at this point were free to do anything you desired.

There had been a lot of complaining coming from the people in tower One. Or so in your delusional state, you thought so anyways. So, you alone made the decision to kill them all off. You told us that it was you, Dave, and joe that had decided to do it, along with you, in addition, you had said to us, that it was because of lack of food, but that wasn't the case at all now was it. Keep in mind that we read your journal entry. You wrote, that as they started to die, you simply laughed at their suffering. You in fact got off on it, and you were glued to the cameras the entire time that this had taken place. You watched on as they had slowly expired. You stayed up for days as you watched on with real delight. You wanted to send fear to the others, you told them what you were doing, and if they got out of line, you would do the same to them.

And it was at this point in time that you found yourself now completely out of medication. But you felt that you no longer needed it anyways, that you were just fine, but you were far from being fine, now were you. You had gone bat shit crazy!

Then you literally wanted to kill off another tower. You thought it had been so much fun the first time. You wrote that you were completely bored. You really enjoyed killing off tower two. Afterwards, everyone still left alive was deathly now completely afraid of you by this point. They knew to not even look at you wrong. And rightfully so. You cared your gun around with you, were ever you went. And you enjoyed this commanding power you held over them. For fun you would go up to them and stick a phone to their head. Get them to cry. You started making them beg you for their food. You enjoyed humiliating them. It was pure entertainment. You sometimes made them do some pretty disgusting things in order to get there food.

Now when the water pump craped out on you unexpectedly. This was not part of the master plan, and you realized than, by killing your brother Joe and Dave you were completely screwed. You have no idea what you were doing. They would have known how to rebuild the pump engine. Oh, You attempted to, but it didn't hold up long afterwards. You knew it wouldn't. That was the real reason why you stored up as much water as you could.

So, you weren't counting on losing the water. Which as an unexpected result you lost all your vegetables, and fruits. You had been banking on them to be able to survive long enough. You didn't have enough water to spare to water them. This was the point when you actually started starving yourself. You really weren't banking on it. You had planned on you and your daughter walking out of there alive, both physically strong. You slowly started killing the remainder of the people left in a vain attempt in trying to save you and your daughter. But you had discovered it was far too late to be able to save either of you. You were completely screwed.

Your journal entries clearly demonstrated to us that you were really started to lose it. You wanted in the worse way to save your daughter; she was the only one that you had cared about. But you just didn't have the resources to do so. Out of all the murdered you had committed in the years inside and seeing the suicides. The one that really got to you was your own daughter. You were going out of your mind seeing her starving to death. And unable to do anything about it to save her.

Then unbelievably the doors had finally opened. When they did, you kneeled down and cried. You thought that just perhaps you could find some water, and food to try and save your daughter. But you realized it was already too late anyways. She had died shortly before you had carried her lifeless body outside. She died before the doors had even opened. Suddenly the joy of this day no longer had mattered. It was at that moment all the wrong of what you did, had hit you like a Mack truck wasn't it.

The one thing you hadn't known about at the time, was that the missiles never ended up coming. I think if you would have known this, that you wouldn't have left all the incriminating evidence behind in the manner in which you had, to seal your own fate. If you would have just locked the doors behind you, and not run your mouth about 78 other people dying. You just might have had a chance to completely get away with the brutality of what you have done. But you were in the advance stages of starvation, so you weren't in the right frame of mind at the time. I can see it written on your face right now, you just realized that you really fucked up. And that you realize that you are now completely screwed. And now Robert your up to speed.

The world is going to see you as the deadliest serial killer in the United States. They will see you for the monster that you truly are.

"I guess so, you know detective. I found out from Dave that there was no missile attack, as I beat him to death. No, after losing my daughter. Maybe, I just had wanted to be found, I'm not really sure why. I just knew that I couldn't do it anymore.

So that being said Robert, at this time, I am formerly placing you under arrest for first degree murder of seventy-eight individual accounts.

Unlawful imprisonment. And reckless endangerment. I personally hope you fry for what you have done to all those poor people.

Agent Robey came and placed handcuffs on me. For now, you will remain at the hospital to recover. But now, you will be handcuffed to your bed, and there would be an FBI agent who will be guarding you twenty-four hours a day. One more thing Mr. Hummel, I personally hope that you fry for what you have done. None of them deserved what you had done to them, being rich or not!

Your right agent Robey, I do deserve to fry!

CHAPTER TWENTY-SEVEN:

"The Big Decision"

April 5th, 2029:

   I was now currently sitting on death row for my many crimes. My execution date is set for April 10th. At 10:30 pm, 2029. Once my bi-polar medications started working again, and my mental state had stabilized. I had realized the horrible things I had done during those dark times, and I went ahead and plead guilty to all my numerous charges leveled against me. My attorney could have gotten me life in prison on reason of insanity. But after having a whole lot of time, to reflect and think, and truly realize the true scale of the horrific things That I previously had done. I have concluded that I truly did deserve to die, so I asked my attorney not to fight for it. I wanted no mercy shown towards me, I didn't want to drag it out, longer than it needed to. The families that I had harmed, needed to finally see justice served for their loved ones that were no longer alive. Though I was nervous about the rapidly approaching date of my upcoming execution. But at the same time, I'm also very relieved. I'm so ashamed for what I have done in the past, and I'm completely haunted by all their faces of the lives that I have taken. Every moment of every day I have been being haunted by the memories of my crimes. The best thing that I can do for all those poor people's families, is to give them a small measure of real justice, and then just maybe with my execution, they will be able to finally find some closure once and for all.

I really wasn't sleeping much. I had just gotten done reading from the bible; a priest here had given to me when I had first arrived here on death row. I started praying soon afterward. I had never been spiritual before all this. I was raised as a catholic, but I'm not a practicing Catholic. I haven't been since I was a child. I'm not exactly sure why was I searching for forgiveness. Not after what I had done. I can't exactly say what had happened. But I know something happened after I had ended up closing my eyes to try and get some sleep.

Suddenly I heard a stranger's calm soothing voice now speaking to me. "Robert, I can help you if you so seek it!"

I opened my eyes, "who are you, wait how did you get in here? And what could your possible help me with. In case you don't know Mr. I'm going to be executed in a just couple of more days from now."

"I know that Robert, that's precisely why I am here now with you. What if I was to say that I could help you through all this? Would you freely except my help that I'm offering you?"

"Wait just a minute, You never told me who you are? And how exactly did you get in here. My cell door is closed, and I never heard it open. And what could you possibly help me with at this point Mister? I'm completely screwed. Besides I don't deserve any help! Don't you know that I'm a horrible person."

"Never mind who I am Robert, you will figure that out all on your own, once you can except the truth. It will be then you will know how I got in here. If I could help you, would you except my help? Even if I offered you absolutely no physical proof whatsoever that I could help you?"

"Whoever you are, I'm going to be executed in less than five days from now. How could you possibly now help me? Don't you know the horrible things I have done. What are you going to help me escape or something, if that is your grand plan, then don't even bother, I just want to get this all over with once and for all. I don't have a desire to escape my punishment, I in fact welcome it. I need to answer for what I have done. I am so ashamed by my actions."

"Robert what if I said to you that I could make all this simply go away, including your overwhelming pain, and guilt for what you have done. All your sins! Your execution, you never having killing anyone, for that matter you never building the bomb shelter. Which started all these cascading of horrible events for you. I could reverse all that. So, say if I could do all this, you wouldn't be a killer, and if I could take all these horrible memories away from you forever. Let all the people that you killed live once more. Would this be something that you would even want. You had just prayed for forgiveness did you not. That is why I'm here now. I heard you're pray."

I was a little weirded out by my sudden presences of this visitor. I was seriously wondering if I was making this stranger up in my head or not. These days I can't be a hundred percent sure.

"How did you know that I had just prayed? Listen Mister, if you could do what you claim that you can do for me, then yes, I would welcome this in a heartbeat. I just don't see how you or anyone else could possibly do something like this? That would be impossible."

"Robert if you want my help, then all you have to do is ask for my help, but you must have blind faith. If you want my help, then you must have faith!"

"I guess, yes I will except your help!"

"Robert, I can only help you, cast you of all your sins of those five years, is if you are fully willing to give up ever meeting your wife, or never having your daughter. Including their memories. If you still choose to ask for my assistance, you must sacrifice your love for her, and the memories of her, and your daughter. If you do this. I can help you."

"If she had a chance to survive and live a happy life even if it wasn't for me. I mean I ended up killing her, and my daughter. Yes, absolutely I want your help then."

The guard was walking by my cell, "Robert who are you talking to?"

I was about to answer him back, when I looked over, and the stander that was just with me, was no longer there present with me. Where did he go, I had wondered. "No one sir, just myself!"

"Ok try and keep it down! Lights out in an hour."

Once he was gone, the stranger immediately came back once again out of thin air it would seem. "Robert, you're the only one that can actually see me."

"Mister are you a just figment of my imagination? I am bi-polar, I do hear voices, and occasionally I do see things that aren't really even there. Is that what this all is."

"Robert, I ensure you that I am not a figment of your imagination. I'm asking you to have blind faith."

"Ok, I know that I am in a very bad dark place, I am asking for your help please."

"Robert what's going to happen, is I will take you back in time, in a slightly different parallel universe, before you ever started the bomb shelter, all the memories of the past eight years will completely be erased from you permit memories. You won't have to be haunted by these memories any longer; you never again will consider building such a bomb shelter. Cindy and all the others will all live their lives once more, as if nothing had ever happened to them. Having never met you. And they will all have a chance at their own happiness once more. You have a chance to be relieved of your sin's, and be forgiven, and have a chance at experience true happiness once more."

I started to cry, "I want nothing more! I want forgiveness. I don't desire to be haunted by these memories any longer."

"Ok Robert you are being given a second chance, do good with it, don't waste this opportunity that I am offering you now, do good with your life. You will be left with no such painful memories of the past eight years."

"So, when is this going to be happening?"

"Robert, you need to remain faithful through all this, as hard as its going to be on you, your faith will truly be tested through this process, beyond what you can even imagine. You will experience more pain than you could ever imagine is humanly possible. The only way that I can help you, is if you must actually go to the electric chair, and right before you die, you will say be reborn in sorts. I can only help you if you have complete faith through this. No matter how bad the pain becomes for you, how scared you become. I must warn you Robert if you don't believe, truly believe, I will know, then I won't be able to help save you. And you shall die then and there on the chair. So, at this point, I need you to believe in the good lord. Do you believe Robert?"

"Yes, I believe!"

"Now Robert, your faith will be tested up until this final moment, You must remain focused, and faithful, believe, and you do this, and your horrible sins shall be cast from you. I must go now, but I will be keeping a close tab on you. You're not alone."

Then this stranger with no name, simply disappeared directly in front of me. Into thin air he simply vanished. Afterwards I had realized what a strange visit that was. But then considering what was going to be happening to me, I have nothing to loss here. Knowing what I know about the rapidly approaching coming events, that I have a way to right a huge wrong that I had inflicted. Talking with this stranger, it did slightly lift some of the weight on my shoulders, of my guilt, and pure shame. I had a way to give every one of those poor people I had killed a new chance to survive.

The day before my execution was to happen. I was asked by the head guard in the death row wing, what I had wanted for my last meal. I had thought about it a moment, then it had come to me. I knew exactly what I had wanted for my last meal.

"Sir, I know exactly what I would like to have, I don't want anything at all, I don't deserve anything, not after making all my victims suffer so much Sir. I starved them, so how could I possibly requestion something special to eat."

"You know Robert, I have been a death row guard now for twenty years, and almost all the inmates tell me how they are not guilty. You since the very first day you were brought here to us. You have fully accepted your guilt; you have been very respectful, never asked for anything more than we provided you. That say's a whole lot. I also know that you had been off all your meds during that horrible dark time of your crime. So, you weren't in your right frame of mind. I am certainly not excusing you for the horrible crimes that you committed. You're the worst murder we have ever had here. But I do respect you for at least owning up to what you have done. Anyways we will be here tomorrow night at 10 pm to collect you and then we will prepare you for your execution. Do you have any questions for me?"

"No Sir, that you!"

He then walked off. I spent the remainder of my time reading from the bible, I caught a couple of hours of sleep, somewhere along the way. As the time grew near, I won't kid you, I was really growing quite nervous, and scared. I guess that this was normal to be feeling this way. I felt like throwing up.

My time was now up, The guards were now standing directly in front of my jail cell. "Open up cell three! Then the door cell slide open. My heart started beating faster, as I realized that this was actually it. My throat became extra dry. It's time Mr. Hummel. Stand up for me please. Now arms out in front of you please." The guards then preceded to then placed handcuffs on me. Then they place leg cuffs on my legs. Come with us. I started walking down the row. Along with three prison guards. The chains on my feet clanged on the concrete I was walking on. And made it awkward to walk with shackles on my legs.

The other death row inmates started all saying, "dead man walking! We have dead man walking here!" it was a tradition that fellow death row inmates did for the one that was about to be executed. It was meant as a sign of respect. I nervously glanced at each one of them as I walked by each of them.

   I was led into the room were the electric chair was positioned. I was directed to go sit in the chair. Then as soon as I sat down. The guards preceded to then begin to prepare me for my execution. The toughest part of all this for me, surprised me, was having to look through the window and facing the family members of the people that I had murdered. I could feel their anger written in all their stares, a few were crying. I knew that there was nothing that I could possibly say to any of them to make them feel any better, Whatever I would say, would be meaningless to them. So, all I could do, is give them what they came here to see. I couldn't let them down now.

   They first preceded to removed my hand cuffs and leg cuffs. They then used leather straps to tightly strap my legs and arms down to the chair. They then shaved a bald spot directly on the top of my head. Then they wet a sponge. And then placed it on the top of my head. On the new bald spot. Then the guard strapped a helmet on the top of my head, and the wet sponge. This was for transmitting the electric volts all through my entire body. The only thing left was to place a hood over my head. A priest then came in the room. It was the same priest that gave me the bible, "Mr. Hummel, do you have any last words that you would like to say?"

"Yes, I do not ask any of you for forgiveness. What I did was absolutely horrible, I realize that now. I am truly ashamed. I am truly very sorry, but I know that's not nearly enough for what I have done to all of you. The only thing that I can do at this point for all of you is dying here tonight. This is the only thing that I can do for all of you. I hope that you can all eventually find some sort of peace. I am so truly sorry! Ok I'm done."

The priest then said a pray. I silently prayed with him. When the priest was finished, I took one last look at all of the witnesses. A guard had me bit down on a leather bit, and then they put a mask over my head. It went completely black. I started freaking out! Then I remembered what the stranger had told me. I started controlling my breathing. I started to silently pray again; this was actually helping to calm me. There was silence around me. The warden just stood there and somberly watched the clock. At exactly ten thirty, he would give the signal. I spent the last seconds of my life praying and doing my best to keep my faith through all this. I would be lying if I didn't say that I wasn't absolutely terrified.

"Then the warden said, "you my precede."

The guard lifted up the power lever, Suddenly I was instantly being introduced to more pain than I could even imagine even possible for a human to feel, or experience, certainly withstand. I instantly literally could feel my blood starting to literally boil inside my veins. My muscles started locking completely up. My body became very ridged. My body wanted to lift up off the chair as my muscles locked up. All I could see was pure whiteness. I could literally smell the smoke, as my body began burning from the inside out. I could feel the pressure building up inside my eyes. As the fluid in my eyes began to boil. They were getting ready to explode. I could feel the life inside me now quickly slipping away in me, My mind so overloaded that no more thoughts were happening. It was just a second at most, just when I was about to pass on. I heard a soothing familiar voice say to me, "It's time to go Robert my child, to be forgiven, and be given a second chance. Cast your sins behind.

As I re-woke, reborn, or whatever you want to call it. I was drinking coffee siting out on my deck at my own house, enjoying the weather. I had absolutely no memories of the past eight years. Including no memories of my wife or daughter. I also no longer was Bi-polar. I was really given a true new lease on life. And even though I had no idea of this previous life that I had lived. It still had forever changed me in unforeseen ways, in a good way I like to think. In this timeline, I was a much more giving, and a more patient person. Making as much money as possibly wasn't as important to me as before, as it once was. I took pleasure in helping others who had needed it. Without being Bi-Polar I looked at the world much differently in a better positive way.

A couple years had passed. I would end up retiring, and my brother Joe would take over and run the company. I truly have had a whole new lease on life.

Here's the funny thing, while I was walking alone down on the beach directly below my house, I surprisingly ended up unexpectedly running into a very beautiful woman walking alone the beach. I spotted her and was quite intrigued by her. I went completely out of my comfort level, I hadn't dated since losing my wife to breast cancer. I went ahead and said hi to her. We quickly had hit it off, I instantly felt like I had just met my soul mate, and her the same towards me. As it turned out I was blessed to meet, and quickly fall in love to yes, Cindy all over again, She too was a different person, she came from a middle-class family. She was a second-grade schoolteacher down in Coupeville, here on Whidbey Island. There was certainly instant chemistry between the two of us. We dated for a couple years when I had excitedly asked her to marry me when we had hiked up to the top of Mount Pilchuck. Lucky for me, she had said yes. We were married a year later, and a year after that, we had a beautiful baby girl. So, in the end things really had turned out for me. I guess I was fully forgiven and blessed.

CHAPTER TWENTY-EIGHT:
"The Hospital"

    Cindy wouldn't barely leave the hospital, she stayed by my side day and night. It was everything that her mom could do to just get her daughter to go home take a shower and change her closes. She just was so worried about me, as any parent naturally would be, also complicated with the fact that Cindy was extremely pregnant at the time, and she needed to still take care of herself. Her doctor was concerned about her getting stressed, it wasn't good for the baby.

    As it would turns out, I was involved in a rather bad accident. The helicopter I had been flying out to the site on. Had unexpectedly had crashed in extremely bad weather. The pilot hadn't managed to have survived. I had gotten pretty badly banged up. The doctors weren't giving me very good odds that I was going to even end up surviving, when I was first brought to the hospital. And if I did, I in all likelihood sustained some pretty bad possibly life-threatening injuries. They stabilized me the best that they could.

Both my legs and ankles were completely shattered in the accident. So badly the surgeons had to install several pins, and screws to put my legs back together. I broke my right arm in three separate places. I also broke my wrist. Broke my collar bone. Broke eight ribs, I ripped all my stomach muscles on my left side. I broke three vertebra. I had a collapsed right lung. Ruptured my spline. Received several deep lashes. Resulting over a hundred and eighteen stitches in as a result. Sustained severe head injuries. Smashed my face to the point that I had to have three titanium plates installed in my face. I had to have brain surgery to relieve pressure on my brain. I nearly lost my left eye. I also had received second degree burns. I have already had six emergency surgeries trying to just save me. And have more surgeries to come. And I am currently now in a comma, and I'm currently unable to breath on my own. I have been here for the last month.

Cindy's parents desired the best doctors working on me. They wanted me to have the best chances possibly at being able to survive. So, I was air lifted from Wichita Kansas, all the way to Cedars-Sinai medical center in LA. Her parents brought in the very best doctors in the country.

Sparing no expense on my care. I was in the intensive care trauma unit. Cindy's parents were trying to be there for Cindy and me. They rented a nice Air B & B within walking distances of the hospital.

Poor Cindy, every day she grilled the doctors on any changes in my present conditions. She certainly was being my advocate. She wanted to know everything that they were doing to me, and exactly why. She barely left my side. Her mom was concerned about Cindy, being pregnant, stressed out and worried about me.

Then in all the stillness going on in my head, I suddenly had heard a very calming soothing voice that was now calling out to me by name. Then I could see them, "Robert, it's time for you to go back to your loved ones now. It's not time for you to go just yet. You have been shown the future, now you know what you must do once you wake up from your comma. You must start fighting for your life, go back. You know what you must do know. Wake up Robert! Cindy is waiting for you. Go be with her."

I slowly then started opening my eye's up. I was rather confused as I was starting to come too once more. My sight was really blurry. I could only see out of my right eye. I turned my head. I surprisingly had spotted Cindy sitting there in a chair beside my bed. She was asleep, and not dead. I was trying to make sense of all this. She looked so beautiful. She was snoring those bubble snores of hers.

    I then started looking around the room. Trying to figure out things in my head. It felt as if I had just woken up from another lifetime. It was an odd sort of feeling. It was knowing if this was real. One that lasted more than eight years for me. I could remember it all as if it was plain as day. I could remember every single day. The best way that I could describe it was the episode of "Star Trek Next Generation" Capitan Picard was hit by a strange beam of light from an object floating alone in space. He had experience planned memories of a lifetime of a memories of a civilization on the brink of extinction. They didn't want to be forgotten about. In the time that he was out, was only like about an hour. He had lived nearly a lifetime, married, and raised kids, he even had grandchildren. That's what this was like for me.

  So how did I get so banged up and end up in here in a hospital. That wasn't making any sense to me at the moment. I was rather confused, to say the least. I was unable to talk, I currently discovered that I had a tube down my throat. I wasn't able to move on my own much. Just by looking at myself, it was clear that I was in pretty rough shape. Both my legs were in cast and elevated in the air, along with my right arm.

A couple of minutes after I had woken up, A nurse had come in to check on me on her rounds. I was glancing over at her as she had come in the room through the door.

She had noticed me now awake again, and she began smiling. "Cindy, wake up, Roberts he's awake!"

Cindy excitedly woke up, and she than immediately looked over at me. I turned my head and looked over at her. When she saw that I was finally awake, she started crying in utter relief, and excitement. "Oh my God you came back to me. Honey, you gave me quite a scare. You have been in a comma. I could tell that she was very excited, and very relieved to see me now awake. God it was good to see her. Just looking at her, she took my breath away. Just like the first day that I had met her. It was nice to know that she still had this power over me.

Then the doctor on duty than came in and began checking me out. He shined a flashlight in my eyes. "Robert its very good to see that your awake once more. Your quite a fighter I give you that. Now I'm going to pull the tube from your throat now. I don't want you to immediately try and talking. Your throat is going to be quite soar." He then proceeded to remove to tube, and then gave me a sip of water. My jaw muscles were rather stiff. My mouth was rather dry.

"Robert, I am Doctor Becker, Do you know where you currently are?"

"At a hospital from the look of it!"

"Do you remember what had happened to you?"

"No, I don't, were, am I exactly?"

"You were in a pretty bad helicopter accident, the helicopter that you were riding aboard, crashed. You were so badly injured; you were air lifted to Cedar-Sinai Medical Center here in Los Angeles. You were in pretty bad rough shape. Frankly Mr. Hummel, I'm surprised that you even had survived the crash. Things may be a bit fuzzy for you for a while. You have been in a comma ever since the accident. And your pain meds we have you on, will keep you a bit grody. Well, I'll let you have some time alone with your wife! We can talk later on."

I first asked the doctor, "Doctor tell me what's the date today?"

"February 8th, 2020."

I couldn't believe it! I got a bit excited hearing what the date was. Now knowing the date, I then looked over at Cindy, I looked at her large belly. Oh my god, She was clearly still quite pregnant. That meant are daughter was going to be born May 21, and 7:42 pm. I hadn't missed her birth. How weird is it too be at your child's birth, twice. I then spoke to Cindy, "I'm glad that I have made it back in time to see are daughter's birth again! One of the best days of my life"

"Wait honey how did you know we were having a girl, The doctor just told me two weeks ago? You were in a comma! And what do you mean again."

"Listen to me honey, what I am going to say now, may completely sound crazy to you, but I insure you, I have been given a pretty wonderful gift while I was in a comma. I was actually shown the future up to eight years from now. And I was given a stern warning. I was blessed with a chance to change the future that I had experienced. They allowed me to come back. And change things."

"Robert you were probably just dreaming is all honey!"

"Cindy, I ensure you that I need you to believe me. I have just lived eight years in time. Eight years into the future. I was in the Comma. I can't explain it to you exactly how it's even possible. I have a hard time believing it myself. Cindy, I saw Megan grow into a little girl! She was definingly a spitting imagine of her mother, in every sense of the world. She had you witty, and stubbornness, and very loving personality. She has auburn curvy natural hair just like you, and green eyes."

"Honey, wait you said that our daughters name was Megan Marie?"

"Yes, that's right, as soon as you found out that we were having a girl, you thought of your dear grandmother. You wanted to name her after her."

"Honey, how did you know that? You were in a comma when I came up with Megan as a name! You and I had never discussed this. And I hadn't shared it with anyone yet."

"I told you Cindy, it's because I already experienced all this all before. You have to believe me. I swear to god that I'm telling you the truth.

   Oh, you know what, I'm actually starting to remember the accident now. The helicopter I was aboard, we encounter unexpected bad weather. A massive thunderstorm bared down on us. We attempted to go around. Unfortunately, We weren't able to outrun it. The weather started getting really bad. He then was going to attempt to set the Helicopter down, but before he could, the pilot started encountering engine problems. After lightning had directly struck the engine. Which fried all the electronics aboard. Then we were hit a second time with lightning. Blowing the rotor blades apart. That's how I received my burns, from when we were stuck with lightning. As we rapidly began losing altitude. He was going to attempt an autorotation, to land us safely without the engine, that was up until there was an explosion in the engine after being struck for yet a second time. Blowing apart the rotors. After that we dropped a couple hundreds of feet in altitude, in mirror seconds, I had never been more scared in all my life. I remember praying to God to be saved. I remember how violent the impact was as we smashed hard into the ground. It felt as if my whole body had just completely shattered like glass. I woke sometime later. Here's the funny part, there was a stranger that was hovering over me. To be honest. I really don't think it was an actual person. They had managed to calm me down. They placed their hand gently on my chest. I was in so much pain. My pain subsided some, as the stranger hand touched me. They said I would be ok, this stranger told me that they had something important to show me. I was told it would be ok. Oh my god, I remember they wanted to show me what would happen in the future, that is if I end up finishing the bomb shelter. Cindy I was given a true blessing because I have a chance to change everything that I have seen before it's too late. Oh my God, I still have time. Cindy, I have a chance to make everything right once again. I cannot let the future I lived come to pass."

What happened, what did you experience. Honey, I will tell you, but it's much too painful to face all that right now, I will say this much, that it was absolutely horrible, a complete nightmare. I will tell you, but not until I'm ready to talk about it. Wait, Cindy does that mean you actually believe me?"

"Yes, I think I do, so then exactly how can we change what you had experienced?"

"We need to stop the bomb shelter completion. We have to refund all the owners. We need to wash ourselves of the whole thing. I know it means we will end up losing a whole lot of money if we do. Especially all the money we spent building this, but if we don't stop this really soon. I promise you; everything will be truly lost. Honey If you believe me, like you say you do. I am going to really need your help with this. This could wipe us out financially! People are going to think that I am completely off my rocker. But at least I won't have to loss what's really most important to me. I really don't care losing everything if it means I still have you and are daughter in my life."

"Robert, I see the fear written on your face, your absolutely serious about all this, aren't you?"

I am, and I really need you to have blind faith in what I'm saying is the truth. In my time, at one point while I was experiencing all this. I was asked to have blind faith, and If I did, I would be given a second chance at life. I believed that I had to die and believe, have faith that it would all work out, and I would truly be saved. I suffered the most painful death one could possibly experience. Now I want to not waste the gift that I have been given. I actually have a chance to save us all this time around. I need to make things right. It had all gone so wrong.

"Cindy, where's my brother Joe?"

"He's back home, running things for you in your absences."

"Honey, please call him, tell him I'm awake, and I'm asking for him."

"Ok sweetheart, sure thing!"

"Honey, I'm getting really tired now, I'm going to go to sleep. Please don't tell the doctor about what I told you about, they'll just think that I'm crazy! I love you! Honey, don't worry, I'll be fine, do me a favor, please go get some sleep in a real bed, you look completely exhausted sweetheart. Think of the baby!"

The next day when I woke up, I looked over and surprisingly there was Joe now sitting there by my bed side. God I was relieved to see him.

"Oh my god Robert, it's so good to see you awake again, we really thought we were going to loss you!"

"Joe, I really want you to know you mean the world to me, you may have a hard time believing this, but I look up to you. I know that I never say it to you, But I love you little bro. I really do appreciate that you have always had my back, thank you for that. I think I need to start listening to you a bit more."

Joe had suddenly got a little chocked up; "I love you too. The thought of losing you was crushing me. Losing Dad and mom in a car crash, I couldn't lose you too. And certainly not in another bloody crash."

"You're not going to loss me little bro, Joe I know that you're going to think that I am absolutely crazy after I say what I need to say to you. Especially since this was all my wild idea in the first place. And I had convinced you to go along with my grand plan. Joe I was completely wrong about the bomb shelter. I need you to understand I had made a huge mistake. Joe, we need to completely abandoned the bomb shelter project now. We can't finish it, I tell you. I'm begging you please; I know it would mean losing millions. If we do. But trust me, you don't want to see what comes to pass if we are don't stop the project now, trust me, I have. Cindy and I will cover all the losses we encounter going through this. You won't loss a dime, but I'm begging you brother, to please do this for me now. Your my business partner. We must stop it! Everything will be lost if we don't."

"What, why would you want to do that for?

It was at that point Cindy got out of her chair, seeing where this was now going, and she reached out and gently held Joes hand, and looked softly into his eyes, "Joe your brother really needs you to do this. I know this sounds completely crazy to you at the moment, but I think while he was in a comma, something weird had happened to him, it was a spirt, an anger, time traveler or some kind of being had come to visit him and showed him what would happen if he continued on with the project. I think though he hasn't said it to me, I think that we all end up dying. And that is why he is so scared now."

I started to ball. If you don't stop this, I will loss you all, when we take shelter inside, we think that World War Three had just started on June 7th, 2023. Five years we were locked up, trapped inside that hell hole we build. You all die. Joe, please stop the project, shut it down! I just can't let this happen to us again, not knowing what I now know. That would even make it worse."

"Joe, I believe him, he told me things that happened, that he couldn't of possibly have known about, stuff that happened while he was in the comma. The only way he could know is in less he had actually been there before."

Joe was looking a bit skeptical at this point, Then to prove to him, that what I was claiming was real actually had happened to me. "Joe how's my nephew's arm, it was his right arm he broke right, don't worry he will still be able to pitch, when it heals."

"Wait how did you even know about that! Did Cindy did you tell you about him?"

"No, I swear!"

Ok then if you have seen the future then prove it, tell me something that Cindy wouldn't know yet."

"Oh, I think I got it, you just found out I can't remember it was yesterday, or today perhaps, that's not really the important part, But I know that Catherine's pregnant again. You just found that out. And you haven't told anyone yet. Oh, Joe, you're having a daughter, you should see her. She's such a pretty girl, she's so full of spirit, oh yay, she has the same birthmark as her mommy, they look like a set of lips on her hip. In the very same spot as Catherine's. You joked with me, that she was kissed at birth."

"Robert how did you know that, and how did you know about Catherine's birthmark?"

Because little bro, you told me about it, the very night your beautiful Daughter Becky was born."

Joe suddenly turned pale, "My god Robert you're telling the truth aren't you, I can always tell when you're lying, you have a tell. That's why your no good at poker. Ok I can tell your serious about this. So, your saying that if we don't do this, we are all going to end up dying?"

"I'm afraid so! Along with everyone else that goes in the shelter with us. But if we stop the project, the future that I experience won't come to pass, and we will all be saved. I just don't care about the money anymore. My family worth so much more to me."

Joe was silent a moment, and then said, "I'll do it, I'm just happy to have my big brother back with us. I'll have to get our attorney involved. Cindy I'll need your help with this as well. You have to help me get out of all these contracts."

It felt good hearing this. I ended up falling asleep upon hearing this news. I felt very relieved. While I was out, Cindy and joe came up with a plan. In the end it cost Cindy and I about 150 million dollars, including giving all the money back to get out of all this, I didn't ask her too, but she covered it all. With money from her trust fund. I'm very thankful that it was now all over with. We could finally move on with our lives. Joe went one more step further. He had hired a demo company to destroy the project. So, no one else would use it either. He didn't want to chance it.

I would end up spending many more months in the hospital, receiving three more surgeries. Then more than six months in rehab to try and be able to be able to walk again, and all on my own. I also needed to do rehab on my right arm, and shoulder.

Meanwhile, while I was still in the hospital, our baby girl was born. Cindy's mom has been a real god sent. She came out to stay with Cindy full time to help her out with the baby. So, Cindy could also be there for me. I required quite a bit of assistance. And Cindy was there helping me.

It was nine months after waking up from my comma. That I was finally being released from the hospital, and finally getting to go home to finish my rehab up at home. I was so excited. I still had several more painful months of healing to still do. I much rather heal at home. And be able to spend my time with my daughter, and wife. I was so relieved to finally be going home. And we lived happily ever after. That really has a very nice ring to it now, doesn't it?

At least that was how I would have liked this story to have all ended! One that I had a chance to be redeem for my many sins. Change the future. Truth told this wasn't any kind of fairy tale Disney movie, things don't always work out in the end like we had wanted it to. Like in my case. Truth told none of this had ended in this manner. But rather not by even a long shot. You see I had been barely clinging onto life at the moment.

Know at this very moment, I'm actually laying on my back, laying on the cold concrete floor, in total darkness, hovering close to death. I'm the only one of us that still possibly alive. Truthfully,

I'm pretty sure. Eight of the other workers that had been with me, had surely perished already. I can't hear any of them any longer. I was able to hear some of them screaming and moaning earlier. I'm so delirious, I don't know what's even real, and what's not real any longer. I can't trust my own mind at this point, it seems to be playing all sort of weird tricks on me. I knew that I was in really rough shape. I thought of Cindy as I was taking my last breath. A tear streamed out of my eyes, before subsuming to my injuries.

It was several hours before the rescuers had finally managed to reach my lifeless, mangled, crushed body. My dream to achieve something big had in the end ended up killing me. I had tons of rubble piled directly on top of me. The rescuers had to end up digging me out by hand. As the two stories that were being built above me, had suddenly without any warning other than a loud cracking, had unexpectedly without warning had collapsed and gave way right on top of us. The stuff piled on top of me, was a mixture of large pieces of broken concrete, rebar, concrete forms, and various pieces of equipment. My chest had slowly been restricted, making it impossible to eventually breathe. I must had been laying there a couple of hours before I couldn't hold out any longer. The whole time I thought of Cindy and Joe. I worried about them. What would happen to them once I pass away. I shut my eyes for the very last time.

Truth told; the bomb shelter was still early in the construction phase. I had been down inspecting the equipment room when the two concrete stories directly above me, had ended up collapsing down right on top of me, and eight other men and me. The General Contractor had been pushing things to quickly, not giving the concrete enough time to fully cure, before placing all the weight of the next story on top of the concrete of the floor below. Ultimately this was in all likelihood my fault, for rushing him. I was pushing to get the project down too quickly. My own lust for big profits, had ended up killing me, and eight others in the end.

I had survived as long as I had, because I had been right next to a large piece of equipment at the time of the collapse. It had created a very small cavity. That had kept me alive as long as it did. But all that weight had slowly began crushing the equipment. I think it was my mind that had tried to keep me occupied during this time, keeping my mind off of all the pain I was in. But because the pain was so much, things went dark in my mind. My mind couldn't deal with all this pain. I really had hoped to stay alive at least long enough to hopefully see Cindy, and at least be able to say goodbye to her. But I had slowly been being crushed to death! No, it wasn't fair that this had happened. I knew my passing was going to devastate Cindy. She certainly didn't deserve this. I felt so bad for doing this to her. I had been looking forward to spending the rest of my life with her, and my daughter. I hoped what my mind visualized my daughter being like. I hoped it was close. She was quite a girl.

As humans we always search for answers why things happen to us. Truth told there isn't always a cut and dry answer, or the answer that we seek. I blame myself for all of this mess. I really had hoped that I had made at least a small difference in this world, in the time that I was alive. At least I knew the love of two good women, both my first wife, and my beautiful dear Cindy, and I managed to have produced a beautiful daughter. At least I was leaving her in good hands. I guess we should learn to appreciate the time that we are blessed with the time we are on this Earth, and the time that we get to spend with our love ones, and just except things for what they are! And look for the goodness in people!

Made in the USA
Columbia, SC
07 March 2023